SINGED

SINGED

TITANIUM SECURITY SERIES

By Kaylea Cross

ISBN: 978-1493762156
Print Edition

Dedication

I dedicate this book to all those veterans and their families struggling with the battle against PTSD and suicide. A great group I've come across fighting this epidemic is **Battling BARE**. To learn more about them and their brave efforts or how you can help, please check out their Facebook page (https://www.facebook.com/BattlingBare).

Author's Note

This is the second book of my **Titanium Security** series, and I hope you love Gage and Claire's story. I'm such a sucker for reunion/second chance stories, and this one really tugged at my heartstrings.

Up next...Ex FORECON Marine Sean Dunphy and a woman you're about to meet in the pages of *Singed.*

Happy reading!
Kaylea Cross

CHAPTER ONE

Rushing to a last minute meeting early on a Monday morning didn't exactly bode well for the rest of her week. Walking as fast as she could in her four inch heels, Claire was halfway from her car to the front door of the imposing black Fort Meade NSA headquarters building when her cell rang. It wasn't even seven a.m., so whoever was calling probably didn't have good news. With a mental curse she slowed enough to dig through her purse then continued hurrying to the entrance as she checked the screen.

She bit back a groan when she saw her father's number on display and answered anyway. "Hi, Dad. I'm just on my way into an important meeting and I'm in a rush, so I can't talk right now." Her boss's call had woken her from a dead sleep at five thirty and she had less than ten minutes to get up to his office for the impromptu seven o'clock meeting. Whatever it was about, it had to be big. The nervous flutter in her belly intensified.

Her father didn't ask her to call him back later or bother with small talk. "Your brother had a really bad night last night. Won't talk to me. Can you stop by on your way home from work, check up on him?"

Claire pursed her lips and bit back a sigh. Well there was no one else to do it, was there? "I don't know what time I'll be done today, but yeah, I'll stop by on my way home."

"Thanks, honey. Love you."

"Love you too." That was the hell of it, she thought as she disconnected. She loved both the maddening alpha male veterans in her life.

Shoving her phone away, she smoothed one hand over her hair to ensure it was still in the hasty bun she'd twisted it into upon leaving the car, and strode to the entrance of the building. Once through security and up the elevator, she left her coat at her work station and snagged a cup of coffee before hurrying to her boss's office. She waved at Ruth, Alex's sixty-something personal assistant, as she passed and received the same in turn. Outside her boss's closed door she paused to take a deep breath and collect herself, then knocked.

"Come in."

She found Alex on the phone, his attention riveted to whatever he had pulled up on his computer screen in the center of his wide desk. He sliced a glance her way, his silver eyes doing a swift assessment of her before turning back to his monitor. Claire sat in a chair opposite his desk and waited for him to finish, fighting off her nervousness. She checked the clock on the wall. One minute to seven, and she was the only one here. That didn't seem good.

She folded her hands in her lap as she waited, her mind churning with all kinds of unsettling thoughts. Was she in trouble again? Two weeks ago she'd tripped the NSANet while doing a favor for a…friend that entailed her poking around for information that might help him and his defense contract team while they worked a high risk job in Pakistan. What she'd found by pure chance had triggered a shit storm here at the NSA.

That single *favor* had resulted in a multi-agency investigation and manhunt for Malik Hassani, former senior official with the Pakistani ISI, now wanted for his connections with Tehrik-i-Taliban Pakistan cell responsible for multiple attacks there. Including the kidnapping and murder of philanthropist John Patterson, and the subsequent attempts to kill his daughter, Khalia.

At last Alex finished his conversation and hung up the phone, then turned his pale gaze on her. Though he'd just turned fifty he was still an imposing man, a former Special Forces NCO who'd served multiple combat tours in Iraq before leaving the Army and joining the NSA. Right now that steely stare reminded her so much of her father's when she'd done something wrong as a kid, her palms turned clammy.

"We've got a situation," he said without preamble.

Obviously, if he'd woken her with a phone call to bring her in this early. "I figured that. But am I the only one you brought in for this meeting?" Because that might mean really bad news. Maybe she was facing some sort of disciplinary measures for looking up classified info for someone outside the agency without permission.

"The others are with the director right now. They'll be here when they're done."

Holy shit, the director? Whatever was going on, it was bigger than she'd realized. She tried not to let her unease show, glad that at least she didn't seem to be in any sort of trouble with the agency. "So what's up?"

He took a manila file from one corner of his desk, opened it and slid it toward her. "Since you discovered his surfacing in Islamabad, the agency's been heavily involved in finding Hassani. He's still holed up somewhere, nobody knows where for sure, but most analysts think he likely got across the border into Afghanistan. At any rate, as of early this morning the cell he's connected with just became a threat for our national security."

What? Frowning, she took the folder from him and looked at Hassani's picture on the first page of the document. Middle aged, heavyset Pakistani man with deep set black eyes and a neatly trimmed mustache and goatee. She flipped the page and scanned the content about his apparent affiliation with the TTP cell, the recent attack on the girls' school in the Swat Valley, built and operated by John Patterson's scholarship foundation Fair Start. After he was murdered his daughter, Khalia, had gone in his stead, and almost died because of it.

That's when Claire had become involved with everything. Because of their recent history together, a member of Khalia's security team had contacted Claire for the favor that had started this whole chain reaction of events in the first place.

"After they attacked the hotel where Khalia Patterson was staying, a prisoner was brought in to authorities in Islamabad. Name of Youssef Khan," Alex continued.

Claire's eye shot to his. Khan was the guy she'd been checking up on when she'd tripped the system. Her heart beat faster. "What did he tell them?"

"Nothing that's helped us find Hassani so far, but through various ongoing investigations we've learned about a new plot they're hatching. John Patterson had a lot of wealthy, powerful friends, including the current republican senator for Massachusetts who plans to run for President in the next election."

"Larkin?" He'd been all over the news lately.

"That's right. Not only has he just vowed to start a congressional hearing about what really happened the night Patterson died and the subsequent riots that killed American security contractor Scottie Easton, he's also donated a shitload of money to Fair Start and is now serving as its unofficial figurehead. Then last night we got word from the FBI that the TTP cell might be planning an attack to target him here on US soil. A hit like that could involve a large scale terrorist attack on a soft target."

"In Boston?" A big city with so many potential targets, and the senator lived and worked there. If that was the TTP's plan, she hoped authorities could stop any attack before it happened.

"Don't know for sure, but authorities there aren't taking any chances. They've already beefed up security on all public transportation, stadiums and whatever."

Jesus. "So the attack's imminent?"

"Yes."

The room felt a few degrees colder all of a sudden. "What sort of timeframe do they think we're looking at?"

"Could be days. Could be weeks or months."

That was scary as hell, but she still didn't understand what this whole thing had to do with her, other than having found out about Hassani by accident in the first place. She knew Alex would never call her here this early just to give her a simple briefing. "And you're telling me this…why?"

"Because you're about to be part of the taskforce tracking this threat."

Whoa. Not even remotely what she'd expected to hear this morning. "So I'm definitely not on probation then?"

The corner of his mouth twitched in the barest hint of a grin. "Well, this way you'll make yourself even more useful and I'll still be able to keep my eye on you."

Claire relaxed and smiled back at him. Excitement pumped through her veins. Ever since she'd landed a job here she'd been waiting for the chance to become part of something important, be more than just a cryptologist, and now she had one. "What do you need me to do?"

Alex leaned back and folded his hands atop his flat stomach. "As of today you'll be pulled from whatever you're working on to start with the team I've set up. You'll be doing signal analysis, looking at encryptions and whatever else we need. Zahra Gill will be your linguist and help you with your workload when you need it."

She liked the female translator a lot and couldn't wait to get started, make a real difference. "Zahra's great. Anyone else I know?"

"Yeah, a few more, actually."

His cryptic reply didn't faze her because he was legendary for them. No, what worried her was the intent way he watched her. It meant he was working on phrasing just right whatever he was about to say.

"There's something else going on," she finished for him in a flat tone, her excitement dimming.

"There is." He sat up, his eyes taking on a hard gleam that sent a shiver of foreboding up her spine. "Want me to be blunt?"

When was he anything but? "Yes." She shifted slightly in her seat. Maybe she *wasn't* officially off his shit list.

"The TTP cell knows about your involvement with Titanium Security, and they also know you work for us."

At his unexpected words the blood drained out of her face, her skin prickling hot then cold. "Oh," she said in a small voice.

"They've been looking into your personal information. We've been monitoring their activity closely over the past few days and came across some chatter on the Web along with some phone calls."

She swallowed. "Personal information like..."

"Your name, contact information, possibly your address."

Oh, shit. She leaned back in her chair, grateful for the support against her spine. Her house was a rental so to her knowledge it wasn't officially listed anywhere as her residence, but considering people from this same TTP cell included multiple hackers and Youssef Khan had been an engineer, filling in the gaps wouldn't be very hard for these guys.

She struggled to keep her expression impassive as she tried to slow her heart rate. "I assume they somehow traced me through my cell phone records?" With her low level security clearance at the agency, her personal phone wasn't encrypted. Stupid, stupid mistake, using her cell phone for those calls and texts to Pakistan. All because of that freaking favor she was starting to wish she'd never done. Why the hell hadn't she just said no?

Because you still care about him whether you want to or not. She pushed the thought aside and focused on Alex's response.

"We think so. With Hassani being former ISI, there's no way for us to know for sure what kind of connections he's still using. It's possible they traced your calls via the cell towers, but it could be something more sophisticated. Just wanted to give you the heads up. And to make it clear, you're not in any direct danger that we know of. If we heard about a credible threat against you we'd take action, but since there isn't, for now we thought it best you were made aware so you can be vigilant as a precaution."

Claire could hardly process it all. This was the last thing she'd ever expected to hear at this meeting. She eyed her boss, believing everything he'd said. He was a notorious straight shooter, so if he knew something important pertaining to her safety, he'd have told her. "Yeah, thanks for that."

He shrugged. "If it were me, I'd want to know. Even if it wasn't standard procedure I'd still have told you."

She respected that, appreciated it even. Didn't mean she was happy about it though. She pushed out a long breath. "Anything else?"

He opened his mouth to respond but the phone on his desk rang. He picked it up, listened for a second, then said, "Send them in." Placing the phone back in its cradle, he met her eyes. "Rest of the team is here."

Before she could ask who the other members were, someone knocked on the door.

"Come in," Alex called out.

The door opened. A dark-haired man probably in his mid thirties stood there dressed in a navy blue dress suit. He nodded at Alex as he entered. "Morning."

"Morning. Evers, this is Claire Tierney. Claire, Jake Evers, FBI."

Claire half rose to shake the hand he offered. "Hi."

"Hello." Evers released her hand and glanced at Alex. "You tell her?"

"Just did. She's doing fine."

She didn't feel fine, Claire thought as she sank back into her chair and Evers moved past her to another. Her hands were clammy and her insides were in knots.

Alex turned his head and smiled at someone else in the doorway. "Hey."

Claire looked over in time to see a familiar face appear. Tom Webster, owner and head of Titanium Security. Delighted, she smiled too and started to rise then spotted a second man behind him. For a second her heart stuttered but then he came into the light and she recognized Hunter Phillips, the dark-haired and muscular ex-SEAL who was Tom's second-in-command. She'd met them both at a security conference in DC last November, along with—

Nope. Don't even think his name. Don't do it.

8

The harsh planes of Hunter's face softened when he saw her and smiled. "Hey, gorgeous." He held his arms out.

Claire stood and walked into his embrace, squeezing him hard. "Good to see you. This is a surprise." She felt steadier already.

He pulled back, his eyebrows swooping upward. "Alex didn't tell you we were coming?"

She shot her boss a hard look. "No, he didn't. But how are you? You all healed up?"

He moved his left arm around, nodded despite the barely healed scar she could see in his triceps where he'd taken a ricochet during the hotel attack two weeks before. "Good as new."

"Yeah? Glad to hear that. Almost as glad as I am to see you here." It was a relief to have someone here she knew and trusted aside from Alex.

"Good, because you'll be seeing a lot of me from now on since it looks like we'll be working together for the time being."

Claire opened her mouth to respond to that when the fine hairs on the back of her neck suddenly stood up. She darted a glance over Hunter's broad shoulder at the doorway as another silhouette took shape there. Taller than Hunter, and wider through the shoulders. She was distantly aware of the way her field of vision narrowed, filtering everything out but the man who stood in the opening, and conscious of the sudden pounding of her heart.

His face emerged from the shadows as he stepped between the jambs. She caught sight of his closely shorn red-gold hair, those vibrant light blue eyes, and every muscle in her body drew taut.

Gage Wallace.

Seeing him was such a shock that she stood frozen in the center of the room as Hunt stepped aside to make room for him. Silent tension simmered in the space between them and she could feel the others watching her reaction. His eyes were every bit as piercing as she remembered, and though those full sleeves of tattoos on both muscular arms made him look every inch the badass he was, right now all she could think about was how good they'd felt wrapped around her.

For a moment she couldn't breathe, might even have weaved on her feet for a second.

"Hey, Claire." That deep, achingly familiar voice washed over her with its North Carolina drawl, put an instant lump in her suddenly too-tight throat. "It's good to see you."

Was it? she thought sourly. Too bad she couldn't say the same in return.

It had been a little over six months since Gage had seen her last, the longest six months of his life. Claire looked the same—a little thinner maybe, her jaw line a bit more pronounced, but just as gorgeous as she had that day at her place in March when she'd uttered the five words that had blown his life apart like a two-thousand pound JDAM. Just like with the warhead, he hadn't seen it coming, and by the time he'd realized what was happening, it was already too late.

I can't do this anymore.

He'd never forget the words or the torment on her face when she'd said them. At the time he'd been too shocked and devastated to do more than plead with her to not let him go. They'd only been together four months but he'd spent as much time with her as he could despite working several jobs in A-stan during that time. Right from the first night they'd met things had moved fast between them, maybe too fast, and looking back now he realized that had scared her.

He'd told himself she just needed time, some space to figure things out. He'd been rushing her, he knew that, so he'd figured if he backed off she'd realize there was nothing to be afraid of about their relationship and that they were meant to be together. Only time and space had done nothing except help her move on. Without him.

Her gray eyes were locked on him now, shock and a myriad of different emotions flickering there before she blinked and put that composed mask in place. The one he'd give anything to tear away and reveal the woman he'd been ready to give his name to.

"Hey. Alex was just…bringing me up to speed," she finished, smoothing a hand over the silky light brown hair she'd curled into a knot at the base of her neck. Gage didn't miss the slight tremor in her fingers as she tucked a stray lock back into place, nor did he miss the pallor of her cheeks. He knew Alex a little because they'd crossed paths a couple of times back in their SF days. He'd heard what her boss had just said about her to Evers. Alex thought she was fine? She wasn't, and to anyone who knew her well that would be obvious.

It was also plain to him that he was the last person on earth she wanted to see in this room, and that she hadn't had any warning about him coming to this meeting.

Alex spoke up from behind the wide desk. "Okay, since you all know each other and introductions aren't necessary, let's get down to business."

Claire glanced away from him and quickly sat, paying a lot of attention to smoothing out her perfectly straight pencil skirt as she crossed one ankle over the other. The hem of her skirt stopped just above her knees, giving him a clear view of the way those nude-toned pumps emphasized the shape of her sexy bare calves. Just below the hem he could see the shadowed hollow at the back of her left knee, that tender erogenous spot where the lightest stroke of his fingers could put her arousal at a simmer.

He jerked his eyes from her legs when Alex continued.

"Claire knows what's going on and has agreed to be part of the taskforce. Tom, your guys are all briefed and ready to go?"

"They're starting as soon as this meeting's done," Tom answered. "I'll be helping coordinate logistics and things behind the scenes. Phillips," he nodded at Hunter, "is our team leader. Wallace is 2IC," he said with a quick chin jerk at Gage, "and I've got two other guys that were with us in Pakistan—Dunphy and Ellis. They're getting us a surveillance vehicle right now."

"Perfect," Alex said, leaning back in his chair to peruse the group. "Claire, you'll work on everything here in the office mostly, but you'll have to assist in the field from time to time as well if they need you."

"Sure."

Gage watched her surreptitiously, his every sense attuned to her. Her slightly stiff posture told him she was uneasy with him here, let alone with the idea of having to work alongside him on the team. And no matter what Alex said or thought, she was definitely concerned about her safety. She was too smart not to be.

The meeting continued with Alex and Evers reviewing the main players suspected to be involved in the cell, going over logistics and protocol. Everyone read through the files Evers handed out but Gage's attention was splintered between its contents, Claire's absolute dismissal of his presence, and the fact that her fucking life might be endangered because he'd unintentionally dragged her into this quagmire two weeks ago. It didn't matter that he'd only called her for help with their investigation at Tom and Hunt's request; the fact remained that he was responsible.

"So, we all good here?" Alex asked when he wrapped everything up, placing his file on top of the neat pile at one corner of his desk. "Your increased security clearances are already in the works and should be granted by later this morning. Any other questions?"

Yeah, he had a few. "What about the situation concerning Claire? How much do they know about her?"

He noticed Claire looking at him from the corner of his eye, but he kept his stare pinned on Alex. One former SF operator to the other in a *let's-get-real-and-don't-you-dare-bullshit-me* look.

Alex didn't blink. "As I told her, there's no credible threat that we know of. If we hear anything more we'll revisit her status then."

"Does she need protection?" He said it calmly, but with enough force that Alex didn't look away. Gage was well aware that pretty much everyone in the room knew of his history with Claire and that they likely thought he was being overprotective. He didn't particularly give a fuck.

Alex regarded him with that intent stare, but there was no bullshit or challenge there. "Not at this time."

"And if she does at some point in the future? Whose jurisdiction does that fall under? NSA? FBI?"

"If the need arises, we'll take care of it."

Not the clear answer he'd been looking for, but he chose to let it go for the moment and gave the other man a nod of assent.

"Okay then, let's start dividing up everyone's responsibilities." Alex handed out more paperwork.

Gage snuck another glance over at Claire. She was scribbling something into the folder on her lap, studiously ignoring his existence even though he knew she'd been listening carefully to that last exchange. At least his questions had served their purpose and she knew he was not only aware of the possible threat, but that he intended to make sure she was given adequate protection against it. Whatever her feelings about him now, he needed to ensure she was safe. It was the least he could do.

Evers and Tom stood and Gage realized the meeting was over. He gathered his papers and pushed up from his chair, suffering a moment's hesitation when Claire went to step past him and froze. She kept her head bent to avoid eye contact, standing close enough that he could smell the light citrus scent of her perfume and see the pulse pounding in the side of her throat. Either she couldn't stand to look at him or she was afraid to. She might as well have kicked him in the gut.

"Go ahead," he offered, gesturing for her to go first. She swept past him without a word and walked through the door, disappearing down the hall on the way back to what he presumed was her cubicle.

As he was exiting the room, Alex called out to him. "Hey."

Gage paused to look back at him over his shoulder.

"I don't take threats against any of my people lightly," Alex said. "Whatever happens, I'll make sure she's taken care of. You have my word."

Gage nodded once. "I appreciate that." Stepping out into the hallway, he shut the door behind him, let out a breath and met Hunter's watchful gaze. The guy had just shacked up with Khalia, the love of his life, and knew all about Gage's shitty ending with Claire. At least there was no pity in the amber eyes staring back at him. "Helluva way to start a new assignment, huh?" he said dryly.

Hunt clapped him on the back and turned to walk toward the elevators. "Never a dull moment, brother."

Not in Gage's life, apparently.

As the elevator doors slid closed he looked to the hallway Claire had walked down. She might not have anything to say to him, but that was just too damn bad because if they were going to work together they had to clear the air enough to at least be civil, and fast. He'd take care of that right after she got off work tonight.

CHAPTER TWO

S tepping out of his apartment building into the late September sunshine, Mostaffa walked down to his favorite neighborhood coffee shop on the corner. The sunlight felt good on his face as it filtered through the scarlet and gold leaves of the trees he passed, transforming them into blazing pieces of jewel-toned stained glass. Though it was warm out now, the temperature overnight had been chilly and a lingering dampness hung in the air.

The heady scent of freshly roasted coffee beans hit him when he opened the door to the shop and held it for a woman carrying a to-go cup in one hand and leading a toddler with the other. She smiled her thanks and he carried on to wait in line.

At the counter, the barista smiled at him. "Morning, Mo. Usual today?"

"Two of them, please. To go."

"You bet." She took his money and he walked around to wait by the side counter for his drinks. He filled the first one with a good amount of cream and laced the other with four packets of sugar, fit on lids and left the shop.

Partway down the first block on his walk home, his cell phone rang. He stopped to set one of the coffees down and dug the phone out of his pocket. "Hello?"

"Peace be upon you, Mostaffa."

The familiar greeting in that soft male voice punched his heart rate up a few notches. He instinctively glanced around before answering, making sure no one was close enough to overhear. The few people walking near him weren't paying any attention to him at all. "And upon you, peace," he answered, a strange mix of excitement and dread filling him. What did they want?

The man switched to Pashto, signaling this was a business call. "We have need of your trusted services. In regard to recent events we have discussed before."

He meant the events surrounding the John Patterson incident and everything that had happened since in the Pakistan operations. "Go on," he replied in English, so as not to draw unwanted attention. Not that he was really worried about that. He didn't stand out at all here even in this quiet part of town. No one would ever suspect what he was involved in, not even his closest friends.

"There is an envelope in your mailbox which details everything we need, and all the information you require. Once you read it and take the necessary measures, you will need to inform me of your decision. Call me at this number."

"I understand." He disconnected, thinking of all the preparations he'd made over the past two years in order for the chance to be of service to the organization. To his fellow Muslims.

He was so lost in thought he'd taken two steps toward home before he remembered the second cup of coffee he'd set down earlier. Retrieving it, he continued down the sidewalk and turned right at the next corner instead of going left back to his place. Under the glorious blaze of red from the towering Japanese maple planted near the edge of the park, a lone figure lay on the park bench beneath it.

Mo's feet crunched in the dew-damp leaves that had fallen overnight as he approached the bench. The man beneath the woollen blanket stirred at his approach, cracked an eye open and sat up with a wan smile on his scruffy face. Mo nodded at him. "Morning, Neil."

"Mo," the homeless vet answered, eyeing the steaming cup in Mo's hand. "Is it Saturday then?"

"Friday." The holiest day of the week. "It was cold overnight so I thought you could use this." He held out the coffee. "Lots of sugar, the way you like it."

Neil accepted it with a nod of thanks, eyed him with a sideways look. "Why do you do things like this for me? God knows no one else ever does."

"Charity is one of the most sacred tenets of Islam," he explained with a shrug. "The Quran compels us to give to those in need." Over the past few years he'd become more devout in his practices. It drove him crazy that so-called "Christians" walked past this man each day without giving him a second thought, let alone help of any kind. Though he suspected Neil didn't accept charity easily. He seemed too proud for that.

Neil shook his head and wrapped his gloved hands around the paper cup, inhaling the fragrant steam that rose from the hole in its lid. He was probably somewhere in his late thirties, but life on the street had aged him far beyond that. His dark hair was long and greasy-looking, and those dark eyes were filled with ghosts of the terrible things he'd seen and done in the name of service to his country. "Gotta tell you man, after my tours overseas I never thought I'd be friends with a Muslim."

"I understand." *Perfectly.* The irony of their situation wasn't lost on him, but despite his radical beliefs he was first and foremost a devout Muslim and this man was as deserving of help as any other. Glancing away from him, Mo nodded toward the bright sapphire sky and changed the subject. "Nice day today, but it's going to get cold again tonight. You should find a shelter to sleep in."

Neil took a sip of hot coffee, his bearded face transforming into a blissful expression as he savored the mouthful. Swallowing, he said, "Just might do that. Thanks for this. You have a good weekend, Mo."

Dismissed, but not in a rude way. "You too, Neil." The small charitable act boosted his mood even more. He took a shortcut through the park on his way back to his place, walking quickly up the street to his historic brick building. Mrs. Grandham, the elderly lady from the apartment across the hall from him was struggling with the front door when he arrived.

He took the paper bags of groceries from her and opened it with his own key to let her in.

"I hate getting old," she huffed. "Enjoy your youth, Mo. It goes by way too fast."

"It does. How's your kitchen sink these days, by the way? Still draining okay? I can come by and look at it again later today if you need me to." Being the building's superintendent had its perks, including giving him the perfect cover. No one in his building would ever suspect him of being involved with a terrorist organization.

"It's perfect, thanks to you." She beamed up at him as she took the bags with a murmur of thanks and headed for the elevator without looking back.

The mailboxes were on the left hand wall of the foyer. Unlocking his he found a few flyers, the few bills he didn't pay online, and a white envelope with only his name typed on the front of it.

Glancing around to make sure he was still alone in the foyer, he tore it open and pulled the two sheets of folded paper from inside with nervous fingers. The first page listed several addresses for him to check out. Two were close by, in outlying suburbs of Baltimore.

As he got ready to examine the second sheet, he was aware of his pulse thudding heavily in his throat and his palms growing damp. The anticipation was heady, a sensation he wanted to savor. He'd been waiting a long time for this moment.

He took a deep breath and turned the page. The second sheet had a high resolution photograph scanned on it. His target. Interesting, he thought as he studied the image. Not what he'd expected at all. Bigger, more important and complicated than he'd imagined. And below the image, in English, *Eliminate by whatever means you determine necessary.*

Relief crashed over him, so strong it made him dizzy. It wasn't a suicide mission then. Not unless he chose to make it one.

His blood pressure equalized and he tucked the papers back into the envelope. He'd have to burn them once he memorized the information and studied that photograph until it was burned into his brain.

The elevator dinged from down the hall. The old lady was still standing there, waiting for the ancient doors to open. He tucked the envelope into his coat's inner pocket and jogged down the hall, excited to embark on his first true mission and prove himself worthy of the cause. "Mrs. Grandham, wait up. I'll ride up with you."

Claire checked her phone for messages on the way down the elevator to the lobby and found a curt text from Danny.

I'm fine. Don't worry about it.

Sure he was, she thought with a spurt of annoyance, not about to believe him. She'd already planned to go over and see him, but that seemingly innocuous message threatened to suck the remaining energy out of her. She'd had a hard enough day already without dealing with one of her brother's moods.

Coming over. Be there soon, she responded and put her phone away. What she really wanted was to climb into her car, drive to her favorite takeout place and bring dinner home so she could curl up on the couch for the evening in front of a good movie. But family duty called, just as it always did, so the takeout would have to wait.

Outside the sky was lit with streamers of orange and vermillion, the sun painting the undersides of the clouds in blazing red as it sunk toward the horizon. The air was cool, the breeze rich with the scent of damp fallen leaves. She breathed it in and rolled her head from side to side to ease the tension in her neck and shoulders. As she straightened she looked over the rows of cars for her silver compact SUV— and came to a halt so abrupt she had to grab her purse strap to keep it from sliding off her shoulder.

Gage was leaning against a black SUV parked beside hers, his ridiculously sexy tattooed arms folded casually across his muscular chest. To anyone who didn't know him he probably looked like a thug. In reality Gage was a people person with a good heart and a strong sense of loyalty, which was why he'd had such a successful career as a Green Beret. Apart from being some of the best soldiers in the world, they were first and foremost teachers who worked with local populations and trained foreign forces. People naturally gravitated to him no matter where he went, men and women alike. And lord knew, all the ladies loved Gage.

The dark shades he wore prevented her from seeing his eyes but she knew he was watching her intently. She could feel the weight of his gaze from halfway across the lot and it sent an unwanted frisson of warmth through her. Which was the last damn thing she needed.

Head up, spine straight, she strode across the asphalt and wove her way between the rows of parked cars to her own. She'd be polite and civil, nothing more. Because she couldn't afford to be anything more. As she approached she nodded to him. "Hey."

"Hi."

She hit the keyfob and unlocked the driver's side door, every cell in her body hyperaware of him standing so close. She struggled to find something to say, something pleasant yet not personal, since she couldn't just hop in and drive off. Their breakup hadn't been hostile and it had been her decision so she didn't hate him or anything. No, unfortunately her feelings ran more in the opposite direction and she couldn't let him know it. She had to play this casually. If given the chance, she was afraid he might try to change her mind since he'd done that a few times early on in the breakup.

Tossing her purse on the passenger seat, she held the door open and half turned to face him, the gesture letting him know she wasn't planning on chatting long. "So, how was your first day on the job?"

He tilted his head. "Not bad. I'm more interested in how your day was though."

"It was…interesting. I'm excited to be working on the taskforce."

"You've been wanting something like this for a long time."

Despite herself she stalled for something else to say, not quite ready to leave yet. "How long have you known about the taskforce?"

"Four days but we got in last night. I gather Alex sprung it on you this morning?"

"He loves to keep me on my toes." He'd also known that telling her about Gage beforehand would have caused her more stress than she was under now. In a way he'd done her a favor by not saying anything.

He didn't nod or make a sound of understanding. The weight of his hidden stare pressed on her, making her want to fidget. "You worried about what Alex told you?" he finally asked.

What, that a terrorist cell might be tracking her? Just the cherry on top of the mountain of shit her life had become over the past six months. "Should I be?"

"I think it wouldn't hurt for you to take extra precautions."

"Oh, don't worry, I plan to." She'd already increased her vigilance and had a 9 mm in the drawer of her bedside table she wouldn't hesitate to use if necessary.

When a few beats of silence passed, she opened her mouth to tell him goodbye but he spoke before she could get the words out. "Have you eaten?"

She blinked at the invitation. No. Oh no, she was not going out to eat with him and suffer the torture of watching him across the table while being bombarded the entire time with the reminder that they were over. That wound had barely begun to scab over, she wasn't about to rip it off and let it bleed all over again.

Facing him now, six-feet-two-inches of mouth watering, protective alpha male, it was hard enough to remind herself of all the reasons why she'd ended things with him in the first place. Reasons that had seemed so strong and logical at the time seemed more like excuses right now. Their dozen year age difference for one—she was thirty and he was forty-two. That he came with the baggage of an ex-wife and a teenage daughter. That she wasn't ready to be a stepmom to said daughter or give up the idea of ever having kids of her own because he'd had a vasectomy over a decade ago. That she absolutely wouldn't be in a relationship with someone in his line of work. Not under any circumstances.

She shook her head. "I have to run by Danny's place, so I'll grab something later. But thanks."

"How's he doing these days?" he asked, giving no reaction whatsoever to her refusal.

"The same." No point trying to hide it. Gage knew all about her brother's battles, had seen a few of them firsthand while they were together. "My dad asked me to stop by and check on him on my way home. Guess Danny had a bad night last night." There'd been a lot more bad nights than good lately. And she already knew that tonight would be no different.

"Sorry to hear that."

She shrugged, the familiar tightening starting up in her gut whenever she spoke about him. "It is what it is, right? Anyway, I gotta go, so…" She let her words trail off, plastered on a smile that belied just how weary she was and hid how much her chest ached at the sight of him standing there, tormenting her with all she'd given up. "Guess I'll see you tomorrow?"

"Yeah. I'll follow you to Danny's place though."

She stiffened, bracing for an argument. "Not necessary, but thanks."

"I'd feel better if I followed you there."

Because of the TTP thing? For a second she thought about asking him what else he knew, but if there really was a credible threat against her she was sure either he or Alex would've said so. And talking to Gage any longer was just asking for trouble because he'd made it clear when she'd left him that he wanted her back. Right now she was too mentally exhausted to deal with another attempt to sway her.

Rather than stage a pointless argument about it she simply said, "Fine. See you." The man wasn't going to change his mind about following her, so why waste her breath?

Without allowing herself to look at him again she got behind the wheel, started the engine and steered out of the lot. Danny's place was a twenty-plus minute drive from NSA headquarters in the opposite direction from her house. Gage stayed right behind her the entire way there. She shook her head at his protectiveness, although his actions didn't surprise her. While she was relieved about not having to talk to him anymore tonight, it still made her heart flutter to know he cared enough to want to watch over her. She just had to be careful not to give him any false signals or allow him to charm his way back into her life, because at the moment she was feeling weak enough to let him do it.

The cheap and slightly rundown apartment building where Danny lived was surrounded by blocks of others just like it. The wooden exterior's paint was peeling and nothing had been remodelled since it was built in the 60s. Since he lived on government assistance and wouldn't take any money from her or their father, this was all he could afford.

Claire parked at the curb out front and climbed out as Gage pulled up behind her. She offered him a wave of thanks and he raised his hand in acknowledgement. Then to her surprise, he cut the engine.

She stopped on the sidewalk to look back at him. Was he seriously going to sit there while she checked on her brother and then follow her home afterward? She sighed and headed for the frosted glass door at the apartment's entry. Yeah it felt nice to know he still cared, but she refused to let that sway her. It wasn't fair to either of them. She couldn't live the kind of life he wanted.

Facing the prospect of dealing with her brother in a few minutes only strengthened her conviction about never getting involved with a military man, let alone one in Spec Ops. Except Gage had slipped past her defenses so effortlessly she hadn't been able to stop him. She absently rubbed a hand over the dull ache beneath her sternum. Sometimes she thought the pain of being without him would never go away.

The interior of the building was in worse shape than the exterior. A whiff of stale, musty air hit her as the glass front door closed behind her. The ancient elevator always gave her the heebie jeebies so she took the stairs to the fourth floor. Stained and threadbare beige carpeting awaited her in the hallway, the stink of cigarette smoke permanently trapped in the fibers.

At Danny's door she paused to gather herself before knocking, calling upon her reserves of inner strength that Gage's unexpected appearance had already depleted that morning. It took over a minute for her brother to open the door and when he did a stab of pain hit her in the heart. He stood there bare chested, wearing a pair of ripped cutoffs that didn't do up beneath the belly he'd put on from a steady diet of meds, junk and no exercise. His eyes were bleary and bloodshot, a week's worth of growth on his face.

"Hey," he grunted and turned away for her to follow, running a hand through his mussed-up dark hair that could use a trim. A mass of scars ran the length of his middle and lower back, some surgical, others from the IED blast that had started this whole catastrophic roller coaster ride. Time had turned them pale pink, yet though his body had knitted itself back together for the most part, it was the damage hidden inside him that couldn't be cured.

Claire shut the door behind her, steeling herself. Just being here made her feel like the walls were closing in on her, as if the air was harder to breathe. The cracked black faux leather couch in the living room was strewn with fast food containers and of course there were the requisite empty beer cans that littered the coffee table. Beyond that the flat screen TV she'd bought him two Christmases ago was tuned to some god-awful reality show that surely signaled the demise of American society. The kind Danny had railed against when he'd first come home from deployment. How things had changed since then.

Claire wrapped her arms around her waist and followed him, noting the unwashed dishes in sink and on the counter, the pile of dirty laundry spilling out from his open bedroom door down the short hall off the living room. "So, how are you?" Though she could already see for herself.

Danny settled himself back in a reclining position on the couch and gave a sullen shrug, not making eye contact. "Just another day in paradise, like always."

Claire fought for patience and forced herself to stand still. Mere months ago she would've already been running around the place like a one-woman cleaning army, washing the dishes, carting the laundry down to the washing machine in the basement. Anything to stop her big brother from living like a pig, and anything to try to save him from himself or have an excuse to avoid an awkward or confrontational conversation with him. Now that she finally understood that he was the only one who could pull himself out of this black hole, she refused to do any of it even though the state of the place gave the clean freak in her a heart attack. Hence the sullen attitude he was throwing her way, no doubt.

"How's your back today?" she tried in an even tone. He looked more uncomfortable than normal.

"Same."

Bad, then. At least, that's what he told everyone. Claire wasn't convinced that his physical pain level was the true problem these days. Taking a calming breath, she eyed the array of plastic bottles lined up on the windowsill over the sink. Seven different prescription meds, some for pain, one for anxiety, others for depression and insomnia. Several more to combat the side effects of those. Put together, they represented a toxic chemical crutch that had slowly crippled her brother into the human shell he was now.

She turned back to Danny. "When's the last time you ate?"

"'Bout an hour ago. Had some pizza with my oxycontin."

Wonderful, she thought tiredly. And there was the empty pizza box lying open beneath the coffee table as proof. He'd be asleep soon, knocked out by the chemical numbness he'd become increasingly dependent on. "Do you need anything before I go, then? I've had a long day, so…"

His head turned. Those gray eyes so similar to her own stared back at her, haunted by waking nightmares he would never talk about. "Dad send you here?"

"He texted me this morning, yeah. You talk to your case-worker today?"

He gave a bitter chuckle. "No. Why would I? They can't be bothered to do anything that might actually help me. I'm just a spare part they threw away and replaced as soon as I got hit by that IED."

She'd heard the "spare part" speech many times before. Claire resisted the urge to scrub a hand over her face or maybe pull her hair out. In spite of herself she started tidying up the tiny, cluttered kitchen, needing to give her hands something to do. "What do you want then? Company? Want me to stay and watch a movie with you or something?"

The bleakness in his eyes sent a familiar chill up her spine. "I'm not gonna OD again, if that's what you're both worried about. You can go."

Her eyes went back to the lineup of pill bottles on the windowsill. He'd attempted suicide twice already, almost succeeding the last time before Claire had found him passed out and called 911. The ER staff had been forced to pump his stomach twice to get everything out. If she hadn't found him when she had, he'd have been dead within the hour.

Once again she was besieged with the sudden, savage urge to walk over and swipe those hateful bottles off the sill with one sweep of her arm, then smash them to pieces all over the kitchen floor. But she knew that wasn't the answer. Her brother's problems ran far deeper than addiction.

No psychologist, counsellor or social worker at the VA assigned to Danny's case had been able to help him. A year of intensive therapy and meds hadn't helped him; in fact he was getting worse. At this point those pills were an excuse, a reason he didn't have to deal with the rest of it. They kept him numb, kept him drifting in a haze that was far more comfortable than the hell going on in his body and mind. The familiar wave of anger and resentment rose up fast but she pushed it down, kept her cool.

She glanced away from the meds into the living room, to the feature wall above the couch that she and Danny had painted together when he'd first moved in. It was covered with awards and medals from his days in the Army. The hardest one to look at was a picture of him in full dress SF uniform, his green beret tipped at an angle, a huge grin on his face. His fiancée had taken it the day before he shipped out on a nine month long deployment to Afghanistan. He'd come back changed, quieter, but nothing compared to when he'd been wounded during his third tour.

She still remembered the blind terror she'd felt after getting the call from her father, saying Danny had been hit and no one knew how badly he'd been hurt. She'd been so grateful to see him at Walter Reed. They'd all been so optimistic, assuming he would recover fully and be his old self again. Even Danny. Instead he'd become a husk of what he'd once been, a soldier with mental and emotional scars more terrible than the ones that marked his skin.

From his arrival at the hospital he'd driven everyone out of his life, including his sweetheart of a fiancée. Their mother had walked away sixteen years ago and made a new, less dysfunctional family with her second husband. Claire and their father were all Danny had left.

She tried again. "Maybe we should get you out of here for a while, whaddya think? Grab a shower and we can go out to that Italian place you love."

He seemed to retreat further into himself at her words, whether from the meds or his depression, she couldn't tell. "No thanks. I'm tired. Just wanna chill here."

He chilled all day long, every damn day, that was part of the problem. Claire let out a slow breath. She'd come to check on him; he was alive if not particularly pleasant or much to look at right now, and he'd eaten. Her duty was fulfilled. "All right then, maybe another time."

"Yeah."

They both knew it would never happen. Along with the severe depression, crippling PTSD and whatever physical discomfort he felt, it was the moral injury he'd sustained that had inflicted the most damage. Something he'd done during his last tour and hadn't breathed a word of to anyone.

She didn't know whether to shake him or cry. "Okay then. See you later." Though she didn't feel like it she forced herself to cross the room and bend to kiss his scruffy cheek. His body odor was strong enough to make her hold her breath. "Love you." Because she did, damn him, no matter how miserable he was to be around. For some reason she still loved the frustrating bastard he'd become. Or maybe it was because she still clung to the hope he'd get better and once again be the person she'd loved and admired her whole life.

"Yeah. You too."

By the time she made it outside and stepped onto the sidewalk, a sheen of tears blurred her eyes. God help her for thinking it, but sometimes she wished that IED had killed him outright, rather than having to watch him slowly kill himself like this.

The quiet whoosh of a window rolling down brought her head up. "Everything good?" Gage asked, leaning over to look at her through his open passenger window.

What she wouldn't give to talk to him right now, the way she used to. Gage understood about Danny better than anyone. She cleared her throat. "Yeah, fine. I'll see you tomorrow. Thanks."

"No worries. G'night." He did the window up and she didn't look back as she rounded the hood of her SUV and climbed in. She already knew she'd be seeing him long before morning. Because without a doubt he'd be right there in her rearview mirror all the way back to her place. And she was more grateful for that than he'd ever know.

CHAPTER THREE

At seven thirty the next morning Gage pushed open the door of the team's new office space the NSA had put them in. Hunt was already there, along with the two other Titanium employees they'd worked with over in Pakistan, all seated around a large rectangular table strewn with laptops and papers.

Blake Ellis looked up to nod at him, a former Marine Scout/Sniper with medium-toned brown skin and hazel eyes. Beside him sat Sean Dunphy, ex Force Recon NCO and resident computer genius. Aside from Claire, Dunphy was the best Gage had seen with IT stuff. His collar-length black hair was already mussed from him shoving his fingers through it. Staring at the laptop screen in front of him, he muttered a quiet curse and typed something with a series of quick keystrokes.

Gage strode over to take a look at the screen. "Hit a snag already?"

Dunphy typed something else in and responded without looking up. "Whoever the TTP have as an encrypter, they're good. I've been at this since six and can't crack the coding yet."

"Lucky for us the day's still young." He turned his attention to Hunt on the other side of the table, poring over the files spread out before him. "Anything new this morning?"

"Not yet. Just waiting on the rest of the crew to get here so we can divvy up assignments."

Gage helped himself to one of the unopened files before Hunter and read through its contents, re-familiarizing himself with the key players involved with the cell. Most of the names were already familiar so he spent time getting to know the ones that weren't. The majority of the men suspected to be involved were Pakistani, but there were a few Afghans and one from Yemen as well.

He glanced up a few minutes later when the door opened. Alex strode in with Jake Evers, the FBI guy. An unfamiliar woman followed behind him, then Claire. Gage straightened, offered a polite smile when she met his gaze then quickly looked away. She was still tense, and this morning she had shadows under her eyes that told him she hadn't slept for shit last night. Whether it was because of him, the situation with the TTP cell or things with her brother, he didn't know, but he was willing to bet all three were weighing heavily on her. It drove him nuts that he wasn't in a position to do anything to alleviate some of that stress for her anymore.

Alex set his own laptop on the table and tossed his jacket over the back of a chair. "Everyone, this is Zahra Gill." He indicated the slender woman with long wavy black hair and greenish eyes that had come in behind Evers. "She'll be helping run diagnostics and working with Dunphy on breaking any encrypted files we find. She's fluent in Urdu and can handle Pashto as well."

Everyone introduced themselves and shook hands, and Gage noticed Dunphy watching the newcomer with interest. Maybe because now he'd have help cracking the encryption and someone to translate the messages exactly—but more likely because he was looking forward to working with a good looking woman instead of one of his male teammates for a change.

"This morning I received new intelligence about what we're dealing with," Alex continued. "Senator Larkin's got a team with him up in Boston, but from recent chatter we now think the TTP might be setting their sights on a civilian target in another city instead. Possibly Baltimore or DC."

At that, Gage's eyes snapped over to Claire. She was standing beside the closed door, unmoving. Although she didn't outwardly react to Alex's words, Gage knew they'd hit home from the way she swallowed. The pulse in her throat throbbed visibly. God dammit, he wanted his gut to be wrong for once.

"That's all we know so far," Evers added, looking a bit sheepish. "I'll update all of you as soon as I hear anything else."

"Gage."

He turned his head to meet Alex's pale stare.

"A word with you and Hunter?" He tipped his head toward the door. Gage nodded and followed him out with Hunt, unable to quell the urge to squeeze Claire's shoulder on the way past. The cell had been researching her, likely still were. Was she the new target? Her muscles were rigid beneath his hand but she forced a quick smile before he disappeared through the door and shut it behind him.

"Let's talk in my office," Alex said, not bothering to look back at them as he continued down the hall. Once they were secured in his office he sat on the edge of his desk and faced them both, arms folded across his chest. Gage and Hunter dropped into chairs across from him. "So. Claire."

Gage's mind was already working overtime. "The Baltimore/DC thing—is that really all you've got?"

"As of right now, yeah."

His jaw tightened as he considered his next words. "No one knows how they tracked her phone records? No one knows who accessed the satellite feeds?"

"We're working on it."

Gage opened his mouth to say what was bothering him most but Hunter beat him to it by asking, "What are the odds you're dealing with an inside job here?"

Exactly, Gage thought. How the hell else would they be able to trace her so easily?

Alex's calm expression never changed. "I'd say slim, but not impossible. We're looking at that possibility too."

Yeah, Gage bet they were. Along with every other three letter agency in the country. "I want a protective detail on her. Now."

Alex nodded once. "Done, but I don't want that out there for her to know. This stays between us for the time being. Got anyone in mind?" He raised a sardonic eyebrow.

Gage looked at Hunt. "Who do you want?" *Say me. Designate me.*

Hunt's light brown eyes were steady on his. "Can you keep your head straight if I assign you?"

Well, Jesus, if that didn't sting. "Just pair me with her during the investigation so I can keep tabs on her." He'd feel better keeping any eye on her personally anyhow. He didn't want anyone else tasked with keeping her safe, and both Hunt and Alex knew it.

"You keep it on the low," Hunt said. "The minute you can't watch her back and do your job, you speak up. No bullshit, man."

"No bullshit," he agreed, understanding perfectly why Hunt had to say it. Gage's objectivity was going to be sorely tested in the coming days or weeks ahead. But then, Claire had always had the disconcerting ability to shoot his concentration all to hell.

"You need backup with anything, just say the word."

Gage nodded, appreciating his team leader's trust. "What kind of threat are we looking at here?" he asked Alex. "A quick hit? Suicide bombing with a lot of collateral damage?"

"Probably something in between. They're gonna want to do something that makes a statement, we think with a giant middle finger to the US government. If they're really targeting Claire, with her working for us it stands to reason they might try something here. Might be improbable but we can't rule it out entirely. Let's just say that certain measures are already being taken. We're not going to be caught on our heels with this one."

Would be nice if that level of concern was because Claire might be in danger, and not merely in the interest of protecting the agency's rep. While he believed Alex cared about her safety, Gage was too experienced to believe differently of the agency. "Good."

"How you gonna handle it?" Hunt asked him curiously. "Think she'll let you hang around long enough to do the job?"

"If Alex pairs me with her, yeah." Then she'd have no choice and he'd have the perfect opportunity.

The older man nodded, a gleam of humor in his eyes. "Consider it done."

They filed back down the hall into the boardroom at the far end. Everyone was busy doing their jobs. Ellis was on his phone, Dunphy was conferring with Claire and Zahra about the encrypted files in question and Evers was listening intently to them. Everyone glanced up when they entered and Gage could tell from the searching look Claire gave him that she knew they'd been discussing her.

"We've got something," Dunphy announced. Gage, Hunt and Alex rounded the table to stare at the laptop in front of him. They'd broken the encryption from one of the online militant forums the TTP favored. A few lines of what looked like Urdu text filled the screen. Gage could speak it almost as well as a native, but he couldn't read more than a few words of it.

"Zahra?" Alex asked.

The young woman cleared her throat and tucked a shiny lock of hair behind her ear before translating. "'Our contact has agreed to our terms. He has the necessary information to carry out God's work, beginning with the target in Baltimore'."

A charged silence filled the room and Gage's hands curled into fists. Were those fuckers talking about Claire? No one was going to harm her. Not on his watch.

"Who is this guy? Who sent that?" Alex demanded, reading the message for himself though Gage knew the man's knowledge of written Urdu wasn't much better than his.

"Someone from a militant chat room," Dunphy answered, his fingers flying over the keyboard as he tried to pull up more info. "No profile on him…" More typing. "A lot of chatter from him over the past week though. Might be their new spokesman?"

"Where's he located?"

Dunphy pulled something else up on screen, then his eyes shot to Alex. "DC."

Alex straightened as they all absorbed that new threatening piece of information, then started issuing orders. Zahra and Evers took off down the hall to gather the people he'd sent them after. "Claire," he added sharply.

She froze in the middle of whatever she'd been typing into her own laptop and blinked up at him. "Yes?"

"You're working with Gage on this. Whatever personal problems you have with him, you put them aside," he added when her mouth parted in shock. "Understood?"

Spots of pink colored her cheeks. "Yes, sir," she muttered, casting Gage an accusatory look out of the corner of her eye.

Well, that was easy, he thought, dragging out a chair to sit beside her. The fresh, clean scent of citrus hit him as he lowered himself into it. Her spine was as rigid as a flagpole and she refused to look at him. He couldn't let things stay awkward. "Hey," he said softly so that no one else would overhear. "We made a good team once. Pretty sure we can pull it off again here."

She turned her head to look at him, really look at him, and what he saw in her eyes caught him totally off guard. Regret. And maybe even a hint of longing before she masked it. She turned her face away with a resigned nod, leaving him reeling. In all his wildest imaginings he'd never thought she'd missed him. When she'd cut him out of her life without looking back, he'd always assumed she'd moved on and fallen out of love with him. Or that she hadn't really loved him in the first place.

What he'd just seen in her face told him differently and a painful burst of hope filled his chest. He swallowed and shifted in his seat, battling the need to tow her out into the hall and drag the truth out of her, demand answers to the million questions racing through his brain. Why? Why had she done it if she still felt those things for him? But a full frontal assault like that would send her running back behind the barricade she'd erected between them, and then she'd fortify the fucker until he'd never be able to get through it again.

He could be patient. Maybe. If it didn't kill him first.

"So where do you want to start?" she asked him, all business as she pulled up files on her screen.

Back at the exact moment when you changed your mind about us. "Let's take another look at what's going on in that forum. Might be able to get some leads there." It was as good a place as any and right now he was content to savor being this close to her again, to be able to breathe in her achingly familiar scent and drink in the sight of her profile at close range. God he wanted to touch her though.

He watched her slim, elegant fingers hit the keys with a muted click, watched her square her shoulders as the website came on screen. "All right. Let's do this."

Claire might not like being paired with him, but she was a consummate professional and would act accordingly while they worked together. The trick was going to be keeping her close enough to guard her after hours until they could ensure the threat was neutralized. Without her picking up on it, even though she was one of the smartest people he'd ever met.

Yeah, he didn't stand a chance in hell at pulling that off.

My God, had a work day ever gone so slowly before? She couldn't remember one ever being longer.

Claire rode down the elevator with Gage and Hunter, feeling caged in between their muscular builds in the confined space. Bad enough that she'd been paired with Gage for at least part of this investigation, but she knew without a doubt that Alex had taken these two down to his office to talk about her and the possible threat against her. No one had said a word to her about the meeting since and it pissed her off. If she was in danger she had a right to know what was happening just as soon as new information came in. Except she knew

Gage would never hide something that important from her, no matter what. Didn't mean she wasn't curious as hell about what had been said in Alex's office though.

"I'm starved," Hunter said as the elevator passed the third floor. "You guys want to grab a bite together?"

Gage stole a sideways glance at her, probably weighing her reaction. If it had been just him and her she would have declined, but they'd worked right through lunch without stopping and she needed to eat. Hunter would be the perfect buffer between her and Gage and it wasn't like she could avoid being with him anyway. "Sure," she answered. "Where did you have in mind?"

"What about that Mexican place you told me about that time?"

"God, yeah. I could do with some melted cheese right about now." Gage stayed silent to the point that she began to feel uncomfortable. They reached the lobby and the elevator doors parted. She raised an eyebrow at him. "You coming with us?"

"Love to," he answered with a smile that made her heart ache. He used to smile at her like that all the time, so easy and unrestrained. Maybe eating dinner together wasn't such a good idea.

"You guys can follow me." She walked with them through the exit and across the vast parking lot. Gage was parked close to her—not by accident, she knew—and climbed into his truck. When both of them were ready she pulled onto the street and drove to the Mexican place.

They sat in a booth at the window, the men across from her. She wasn't sure if it was worse to have Gage beside her or across from her where she couldn't avoid looking at him. The pale blue button down he wore emphasized the muscular lines of his shoulders but hid his tats. Shame, that. They were beautiful and each bit of ink told a story about what was most important to him. His daughter, his life as a Green Beret, and the men he'd lost while serving his country.

"So, how've things been going?" Hunter asked her as he set his menu down.

"Good. Just busy with work, family stuff." She could feel Gage's gaze on her, knew he read far more into that than Hunter would. "What about you? I heard you convinced Khalia to move in with you."

Hunter's harsh features transformed into a broad smile that made his eyes twinkle. "I did. Couldn't be happier about it."

She smiled back. "That's great to hear. How's she doing? I mean, considering everything she's been through." Her father had been murdered by the same TTP cell that may or may not be targeting Claire now. They'd done their best to kill Khalia when she'd gone to Pakistan in her father's stead to set up the Fair Start school in the Swat Valley. If not for Hunter and the rest of the Titanium team, they would have succeeded.

"It's not easy for her, not gonna lie, but she's managing better than either of us expected. Her therapist is blown away by her positive attitude, her willingness to overcome everything. Still has bad times, some nightmares, but she knows I've been there and that I get it. She even gets me talking about my own shit sometimes."

Claire widened her eyes, because getting one of these Spec Ops-trained alpha males to open up like that was next to impossible. "I'm impressed. And does it help?"

Another smile, so full of love it set off a twinge in her chest. "It does. Never thought I'd tell her about a lot of the stuff, but sometimes I need to. She listens. Makes it easier that she's seen too much shit herself, because I know she understands where I'm coming from most of the time."

"I'm so happy for you." She truly was. "Think I'll ever get to meet her?"

"She might come up for a few days before she heads to DC for a conference next weekend. We've started up a foundation for a buddy of mine we lost the night of the riots in Pakistan."

"Scottie Easton?"

Hunter smiled in appreciation that she knew the name. "That's him. It's going to provide privately funded counseling, therapy, job training and education for vets suffering from injury or other things like PTSD. Our services will be off the record so no one's security clearances will be jeopardized. It was all Khalia's idea. I'm helping with some of it, and I'm really looking forward to making a difference. God she's amazing." He shook his head, grinned and picked up his Corona, took a long pull. "How's your brother these days?"

She sighed. "Not good. We've tried everything. At one point we thought he might qualify for a therapy dog but they assessed him as not being capable of taking care of one." Looking back, in some ways that now seemed like the tipping point for Danny. Being told he wasn't even able to care for a dog had hit him hard, made him even more resentful. She and her father had briefly thought about adopting a dog and taking it over to see him a few times a week, but never followed up on it. Maybe they should talk about it again. Unconditional love in the form of a wagging tail and velvety brown eyes might help lift some of the depression at least. Or she could be grasping at straws again.

Hunter nodded, his eyes full of understanding. "Maybe we can find someone through our foundation who might be able to try something different. There are all kinds of new ground breaking treatments coming out."

"I'd love that. Dad and I are at our wit's end with him. If you come up with anything, let me know?"

"Absolutely. I'll tell Khalia tonight when I call her later. You'll probably have an e-mail full of resources from her when you turn on your computer tomorrow morning."

"Ah, a woman of efficiency. I like her already." She cast a glance at Gage, who'd been quietly sipping his own beer through the entire conversation, break the ice a bit more. She felt the need to draw him into it. "And you? How's Janelle doing these days? I haven't talked to her in a couple weeks."

"She's good. Her mom's making her buckle down at school and she's on the girls' volleyball team there. She always asks me about you whenever I talk to her."

Janelle was a sweetheart, and not quite fourteen going on twenty-five. Wasn't easy growing up a military brat, let alone in a divorced family with strained relations between your parents, Claire knew this firsthand, yet Janelle seemed to be handling it well. She now lived in Nashville with her mother. "Do you get to see her very often these days?"

"Not as much as I'd like, but things are better between us now so we talk a lot more than we used to. She texts me all the time. Worried about her old man, I guess, no matter what I do to reassure her."

Yeah, Claire knew exactly how that felt. All the stress and worry about her father and brother had been compounded by fear for Gage every time he'd taken a job overseas. That had proven to be the breaking point for her. After what had happened to both men in her family she'd sworn never to live that kind of life again. Not even for Gage. "I'll call her this week. Bet she'll get a kick out of us working together."

The corner of Gage's mouth quirked, drawing her gaze to those sexy lips. God, the things the man had done to her with that mouth. "Yeah, she will."

The meals came and the conversation flowed easily around the table. The way Gage and Hunter ribbed each other made her laugh and miss being part of that inner circle and privy to the easy banter between military men. After they finished eating she excused herself from the table and went to the washroom, intercepting their server on the way so she could pay the bill. Gage and Hunter protested when they discovered what she'd done but she waved it off.

"So," she began, picking up her sweater from the padded seat of the booth. "You guys gonna tell me what went on in Alex's office?"

They both blinked up at her, innocent as choir boys. She wasn't buying it for a second. "Seriously? I can't believe you guys won't tell me!"

"Nothing we haven't already covered with the rest of the team," Gage answered evenly.

Arms folded across her chest, Claire turned her glare on Hunter. "You swear?"

He held up his hands, palms out. "I swear. If there was anything going down, I'd tell you no matter what the NSA said."

Satisfied, she nodded. "Okay then, guess that's all I'm gonna get out of you. See you guys in the morning?"

They both stood and Gage took a step toward her. "You headed home?"

She wished. "No, I have to pick up a bunch of groceries and drop them off for my dad and Danny first. Danny's fridge was empty when I was there yesterday."

He nodded, snagged his keys from his pocket. "I'll follow you."

"You don't have t—"

"Don't bother arguing."

Okay, then.

She headed for the door, both men trailing behind her. She and Gage waved to Hunter as he climbed into his own truck and they continued to where they'd parked side by side. Tension gathered in Claire's belly. She was acutely aware of all the things left unsaid between them, piling up into a wall neither one of them would be able to ignore for much longer.

In some ways she'd have preferred he confront her about the breakup straight out. No way could they work together on this taskforce and dance around that landmine for much longer. But he didn't bring it up. In fact he didn't say anything at all as he walked her to her vehicle and insisted on opening the door for her. His Southern manners were as much a part of him as the fighting skills the Army had drilled into him. It was one of the things she loved and missed about him most.

Standing beside the open driver's door, she almost blurted *Are we going to talk about it?* Self-preservation made her hold back. She smiled her thanks, wished him a good night and allowed him to shut the door for her. When he'd turned his back she leaned her forehead onto the steering wheel and blew out a deep breath. God, this hurt. She was such an idiot to think she could ever fall out of love with that man. What the hell was she going to do now?

His truck's engine roared to life beside her. Straightening, she drove to the nearest grocery store, filled a shopping cart and drove first to her dad's place. He wasn't home, likely halfway through his twelve hour shift at the shipyard. Just as she'd suspected his fridge was pretty much bare save for the requisite twenty-four pack of beer on the top shelf. Not for the first time she was thankful that he was as high-functioning an alcoholic as he was, showing up for work every shift and paying his bills on time.

At the door she paused to examine a framed photo of the three of them hanging on the wall. Her, her father and Danny on the day of her brother's graduation from SF school. Danny looked so handsome in his uniform, so full of confidence and excitement about what the future would bring, her father's smile so proud. Staring at the photo now, her eyes stung. She shut off the foyer light and locked the door behind her.

Gage followed her next to Danny's. At his door she knocked a few times but there was no answer. Berating herself for the jolt of fear that seized her, she set the groceries down and dug her spare key out of her pocket. Her hand shook as she turned the brass knob. Inside she found Danny passed out on the couch, vials of pills lined up next to him on the coffee table. Pausing in the kitchen doorway, she stared at his chest. It was moving up and down. Claire closed her eyes and let out a breath of relief. For a moment she'd thought—

"Everything all right?"

She whirled around to find Gage standing in the apartment doorway. She'd been so focused on making sure Danny was okay she hadn't realized she'd left it wide open. "He's just sleeping," she whispered, the flood of relief draining what little energy she had left. "I'll unpack these and get going. He's not going to wake up anytime soon."

Probably better that he didn't until she was gone, so they could avoid another awkward or hostile encounter. And God only knew what Danny would think about having Gage in his apartment, playing witness to his epic downward spiral. Back when she'd first introduced them Danny had clearly worshipped Gage, and would always respect his status as former SF Master Sergeant no matter what.

Shaking her head, she started putting everything away. Gage moved around the tiny kitchen without a word, helping to straighten up the mess Danny had left while Claire stocked the fridge and pantry with staples. Bread, butter, milk and eggs. Peanut butter, apples and bananas. His favorite brand of cookie. She knew he'd send her a thank you text whenever he woke up and saw what she'd done.

She sucked in a breath as the tears clogged her throat.

"Hey." Large, gentle hands closed over her shoulders.

Claire gave a sharp shake of her head and twisted away, barely hanging on to her control. She couldn't handle his gentleness and concern right now. If he touched her again she would crumble and she couldn't afford to.

Before leaving she stopped at the couch to cover Danny with a blanket. She bent to kiss his scruffy cheek and left him, locking the door quietly behind her. Gage was right behind her. The weight of his stare pressed between her shoulder blades all the way down the stairs to the exit.

Outside the sky was a deep cobalt blue, a thousand stars twinkling brightly overhead. Tipping her head back, she drew in a long breath.

"He like that often now?" Gage asked beside her. He stood close enough that she could feel his body heat and smell his clean, woodsy scent. In that moment, more than anything she wanted to crawl into his arms and have him hold her.

No point in lying. "Unfortunately, yes," she admitted, turning her head to look at him. "It's like he's in quicksand. We've tried everything we know of to pull him out. But now I don't think he even cares if he goes under." It was weird, but in some ways she missed the rages he'd flown into. At least then he'd shown he still had some fight left. This bitter, apathetic Danny frightened her the most.

"Fuck, I'm sorry, Claire. I wish I knew how to help."

A sad smile twisted her mouth, at his sympathy and choice of words. The F bomb was so Gage. He tended to use it like an adjective, didn't even seem to notice when he said it half the time despite his efforts to tone it down around her and Janelle. You could take a man out of the Army, but you couldn't take the Army out of the man, and he'd been in a long time.

"It's okay. Just hard to accept, you know? Seeing him that way and not being able to do anything." She was silent a moment before voicing the dark truth that burned like a coal beneath her sternum. "At this point I don't even like him anymore. Sounds awful and cold for me to say it, I'm sure, but it's the truth." It also told Gage how dire things had gotten without her having to explain in detail. He knew how much she'd revered her big brother.

Twisting away she took a step toward her SUV when Gage caught her upper arm in one hand and turned her around to face him. Hard fingers tilted her chin up until she was forced to meet his eyes. So blue, like an endless ocean she could drown in if she wasn't careful.

"That doesn't make you a bad person," he said forcefully, eyes drilling into hers. "He's lucky to have a sister who still cares about him enough to buy him groceries and check in on him even when he treats her and everyone else like shit. It's like you said, you can't pull him out of the quicksand. He's the only one who can."

"And what if he doesn't?" she whispered, admitting her worst fear.

"Then at least he won't pull you under with him," he answered.

God. Claire dropped her head, didn't resist when Gage slid his arms around her back and pulled her into his body. Slowly, imprinting the feel of him into her memory, she returned the embrace. Warm, solid muscle surrounded her. The horrible weight she'd been carrying seemed to magically ease off her shoulders. She leaned into him, grateful for his presence and that he kept this about comfort only without pushing for more than she was willing to give. Not that she didn't wish for more—she'd loved their voracious sex life. As a lover Gage could be rough or tender and everything in between. She'd never met a man who could make her burn the way he did. The physical aspect of their relationship had never been the problem, however.

They stood like that on the sidewalk for a long time, neither of them speaking, as though they were both afraid of shattering the harmony they'd forged.

Finally she found the strength to draw her head away from his solid shoulder. "Well. Another long day for us tomorrow. Guess we'd both better get some sleep." She lowered her arms and eased away from him, every cell in her body crying out in protest. For a fleeting moment she considered throwing all caution aside and giving into the temptation of running her hands through that soft skull trim, then draw his head down to kiss the ever loving hell out of him. *And ten seconds after that you'll be underneath him in the back of his SUV, naked.*

She stepped back. "Drive carefully."

He nodded, his expression inscrutable, giving her no clue what he was thinking. He'd held her like a friend would, nothing sexual in his embrace at all. What did that mean? Maybe he really had gotten over her and moved on in the past few months. The thought put a lump in her throat, which was crazy because wasn't that what she'd wanted? Although she'd hated to hurt him, she'd known it was for the best in the end.

"I'm here if you need me, okay?" he said quietly.

Just like that. No demands for more, no expectations.

Her throat tightened more, because she knew he would be there for her no matter what. *I love you,* she thought wistfully. *I'll always love you.*

"Thank you." Feeling like she was ripping her skin away, she forced herself to step back and return to her vehicle, all the while knowing she faced another sleepless night spent aching for him in her lonely bed.

CHAPTER FOUR

Mo couldn't believe his luck. Considering who his target worked for, he'd assumed locating them would be much harder. Yet here he was, on the sidewalk across from the tidy brick two-story house in the quiet residential neighborhood of Columbia. All the lawns were manicured, the fallen leaves carefully raked up and placed into bags waiting at the curb for the city crews to take them away for composting. All except the house he was staring at.

Its yard hadn't been tidied up for a while, if the carpet of damp, decaying leaves was any indication. The lawn was in need of a mowing too. As if whoever lived here was either too busy to deal with it, or perhaps they didn't care. Whatever the case, it made the property stand out in this well kept neighborhood. He cast another glance up and down the street. A jogger was headed away from him at the far end. Most of the driveways were empty, everyone off to work or to drop their kids off at school. This was too easy.

It made him nervous.

He'd taken on other jobs for the TTP cell before, little things like reconnaissance or acting as a courier. Never anything as big as this. This was a test, to see if he had what it took, whether all his training they'd provided had paid off. And he was nervous as hell about making sure this operation went off without any mistakes.

A UPS truck pulled away from the curb up the street and passed him. Making sure he displayed confident body posture, Mo crossed the street and walked up the target's driveway. First he needed something to verify they did indeed live here before he went any further with this. For all he knew, that was part of his test too. A newspaper lay on the welcome mat on the front stoop. Through one of the long rectangular windows that flanked the metal door he clearly saw the security system keypad on the foyer wall, its little red light blinking every two seconds.

He recognized the model, and immediately looked up for the motion detectors mounted on an interior wall facing the door. He'd worked for ADT long enough to guess where the other sensors probably were. On the lower floor window contacts and doors. Few people bothered with the upper floor, and that was probably his best bet for entry. Once he got in, he'd be able to discern where the other motion detectors were and figure out how to disable them. Because to do his work, he needed access into the crawlspace. He circled around the house to the backyard, which was in the same untidy condition as the front.

The sound of a sliding door opening next door on the other side of the privacy fence made his heart jolt.

"Hello?" a female voice called out.

Shit. He quickly stepped back and searched for the best escape route, wanting to avoid anyone getting a good look at him. Before he'd taken two steps, a woman next door stuck her head over the six foot tall wooden fence separating the properties.

She held a toddler on one hip and gave Mo a polite smile, but it was obvious she was surprised to see him there. "Hi."

"Morning," he answered, thinking fast. He wore a ball cap and backpack, and the cooler weather excused the gloves he'd worn to prevent leaving fingerprints. He just had to sell her on the idea that someone up to no good would never stand there having a conversation with her like this in broad daylight. "Just checking out the yard. I own a landscaping company. The homeowner called to ask me to come over and give them a quote about cleaning up the place."

"Oh, they don't live here—they're the landlord. The renter left about an hour ago. That's great you're going to do the cleanup though. Whenever the leaves build up out front they clog the gutters and then when it rains hard our yard gets flooded. I've talked to the landlord plenty of times and they never do anything about it." Her annoyed expression softened when she offered him another smile. "Are you going to do the gutters too?"

"I was just going to look at them." Climbing up on a ladder would give him the perfect opportunity to check for an entry point on the upper floor.

"Great." She turned her head to coo something at the blond-haired boy on her hip, then looked back at Mo. "Well, have a good day."

"You too." She disappeared from view and he heard the sound of the sliding door shutting behind her a moment later. He let out a sigh of relief. Nosy neighbors made his task more difficult. The blinds were drawn on all the windows except for one on the upper floor that he guessed must be the master bedroom and there was no way he could see through it without having an extension ladder, which he didn't have. Even if he'd just given himself the excuse to pretend to be checking out the gutters, he'd verified the address and the neighbor lady said the occupant was a renter, so he was positive he had the right place.

The heavy tools in his backpack bumped into his spine as he circled around to the left side of the house, looking for an easy entry point. Over the last day he'd thought of several ways to kill the target; some where he had to get up close, others…not so much. Because it allowed him an easy escape route, he'd already decided on the latter. He had what he needed to set everything up right in his backpack. If he could sneak in he could do it now and carry out the hit tonight. But he didn't like that the neighbor lady might be watching. For all he knew she might be on the phone to the landlord right now to talk about things that needed to be done in the yard. Last thing he wanted was to make anyone suspicious or investigate further.

Then, as if it was a message from above, the first drops of rain began to fall and made the decision for him. They hit the brim of his cap, pattered against the leaf-covered roof. Looked like the lady next door might have a flooded yard in the morning. The wet only increased the likelihood that he'd leave muddy tracks in the yard.

Aborting the plan to go ahead with the setup today, Mo quickly strode around to the front of the house and crossed the street to his rental vehicle. As he drove away through the steadily increasing rain, he was already planning his next move.

Gage rolled up and parked at the curb out front since Hunter and Ellis had already taken up the driveway of the safe house the NSA had put them in. It was just after seven, the sky already dark and the rain had eased off to a light shower.

Normally he'd be out tailing Claire but she'd been in meetings on another floor most of the afternoon and he hadn't heard from her since lunch. She'd replied to his text inviting her out for a bite to eat saying she couldn't meet up for dinner because she had plans to go out with her best friend, Mel, after work.

Rather than look like a desperate ex or tip her off that she needed watching, he'd arranged for Dunphy to tail her instead. It bugged Gage that he couldn't keep eyes on her himself, but he trusted Dunphy. Guys didn't make Force Recon without amazing observation skills, and if any threat should materialize on Dunphy's watch, he could handle it.

Gage let himself in through the front door and found Hunt and Ellis at the kitchen island drinking beer and eating a plate of what looked like nachos. Chips and cheese, nothing else. Gage set his laptop case and shoulder holster down and shook his head at them. "That's dinner? I fill the fridge last night and that's the best you could come up with?"

"Yeah. Feel free to whip up something else for yourself," Hunt replied, stuffing a wad of cheese-drenched chips into his mouth.

Gage strolled into the kitchen. "Okay. You boys're welcome to watch this free cooking lesson, so long as you don't bother asking me for any of it when I'm done."

"Can't guarantee that. Depends on what you're making," Ellis commented, slapping Hunt's hand away from a giant glob of cheese stuck to the plate and stealing it for himself.

"None of your business, is it?" Gage answered, and started digging ingredients out of the fridge. Chorizo, bell peppers, cream, garlic and parmesan. The others continued munching on their chips while he chopped and minced. He'd just put everything in a pan on the stove to sauté when his phone vibrated in his hip pocket. He dug it out and read Dunphy's text. *Zahra just showed up to meet them.*

A moment later, *Best surveillance job EVER.*

And finally, *I love you, man.*

Snorting, Gage put it away and got back to the chorizo and peppers sizzling in the pan. He noticed both Ellis and Hunter were now staring at it like hungry wolves, their half-demolished dinner sitting abandoned between them. "Sure smells good," he said to himself, giving the pan a little shake as he hid a grin.

Ellis sat forward on his stool, taking a closer look. "That's too much, even for you. I'll eat whatever's left over."

"There's not gonna be any leftovers. Maybe you two losers should put in a little more effort next time, huh?"

"Where the hell did you learn to cook like that, anyway? Cuz it wasn't in the Army." Scowling, Hunter picked up his beer and took a long pull.

He shrugged. "I'm a divorced dad. Can't feed your kid fucking nachos and mac and cheese every night. It was either figure out how to cook real food, or risk poisoning my only child." He'd been a piss poor cook at first, too. Poor Janelle. Now his pasta carbonara was her favorite dish and he had a handful of go-to meals that were actually damn tasty. He had Claire to thank for that, at least in part. She'd been the one to encourage him to continue with his clumsy attempts to reach out to his daughter when he hadn't been sure how to bridge the gap between them. Claire had been a steadying presence in his chaotic life, which was why he'd been so crushed then pissed off when she'd kicked him to the curb.

Ellis shoved the half empty grease-covered plate toward Hunter. "Here, have at 'er." A few moments later he was at Gage's elbow, peering down into the pan. "Do that flippy thing again. You know, the…" He mimicked the motion with his hand.

"What, this?" Gage raised the pan slightly and gave a flick of his wrist to toss the contents around, catching them all without spilling.

"Yeah. That's freaking awesome. Bet chicks dig that move, huh?"

"Yep." It had certainly impressed Claire. One morning when she'd come into his kitchen and found him flipping pancakes like that, she'd jumped him right there at the stove, ripping off his clothes and climbing his body like a tree. They'd hit the floor laughing and he'd barely had the sense to reach up for the switch to turn off the stove. That morning they'd missed breakfast and wound up eating the pancakes for lunch instead. The memory of it was bittersweet, filled his gut with that familiar ache he always experienced when he thought about her.

"For Christ's sake, don't drool in it," Gage muttered, elbowing Ellis out of the way. "Grab me the heavy cream over there and two plates."

"Heavy cream?"

"Whipping cream. Jesus, don't you watch the Food Network?" Ellis quickly passed it to him and stood silently while Gage made the sauce and let it reduce. "Normally I'd toss this with some fettuccini but I'm way too fucking hungry to wait for the water to boil."

Ellis nodded. "Word."

When it was finished Gage divided the steaming mixture onto the plates. Ellis went with him to the table and the two of them dug in while Hunter watched. Ellis moaned and rolled his eyes back on the first bite and Gage couldn't help but grin at Hunter's sullen expression.

"Good?" Gage asked Ellis.

"Mmmhmmm," he mumbled around another mouthful, his eyes half closed in pleasure.

In response Hunter narrowed his eyes at them and pointedly shoved a couple more greasy nacho chips into his mouth.

With a chuckle Gage turned his attention back to his plate and polished off his dinner. One forkful from finishing, his phone rang.

"Aren't you the popular one tonight," Hunter remarked as Gage put the thing to his ear.

Gage held up his middle finger as he answered the unknown number. "Wallace."

"Gage?"

He stilled and frowned. The male voice was familiar somehow but he couldn't place it. "Yeah. Who's this?"

"It's Wayne. Claire's dad." The urgency in his voice lit up Gage's inner warning system.

He was up and out of the chair heading for the quiet of the living room without conscious thought. Wayne had never called him before. Ever. "Hi there. How are you?"

"I'm…not good. I didn't know who else to call." The man's voice cracked, sending Gage's pulse up a notch.

Claire was fine, still out with her friends, or Dunphy would've called. "What's wrong?"

A shaky sigh answered him. "I can't get hold of Claire but she told me you were in town. Are you still?"

"Yeah, what do you need?"

"Just… Can you meet me at her place? I need to talk with her and it would help to have you here when I do." He was near tears, the ragged edge to his voice making the hair on Gage's nape prickle. "I'll tell you everything when you get here."

"I'll be there in ten minutes." Gage hung up and raced back into the kitchen to grab his keys. Hunter and Ellis were on their feet.

"What's up? Do you need us?" Hunter asked.

He shook his head. "Not yet. That was Claire's dad. He wants me to meet him at her place. I'll call you once I know what the hell's going on."

Whatever it was, it was bad. On the way out to the SUV he tried Claire's cell but it went straight to voicemail. He texted Dunphy to blow his cover, go in there and tell Claire to call her father. Dunphy texted back thirty seconds later that she'd already left the restaurant and he was following her. Gage hoped she was going home. As for him, he was going to make sure he found out what was happening before she got there.

CHAPTER FIVE

"Thanks for dragging me out tonight," Claire said as she hugged her best friend.

Mel squeezed her in return, her answering laugh warm and bright as a sunbeam. "You're welcome. It's been way too long since we've gone out. I knew you needed it."

"I did, more than I realized. I used to be fun, dammit! Wait, I'm still fun, right?" She pulled back to eye her friend.

"Definitely," Mel said, then looked at Zahra, who was at the curb pulling her long black hair into a clip at the base of her neck. "She's still entertaining, yeah?"

"Very much so," Zahra agreed, hazel eyes dancing with humor. "Who knew?"

"Oh, come on, you always suspected I was fun to hang out with," Claire told her.

She shrugged. "Yeah, I did, but consider the source. I'm a linguist, so not really known for lighting the night up, you know?"

"Well I kind of like that about you." Claire turned her attention back to Mel, who'd spent half the evening digging for details about Gage and the other regaling tales of her own recent dating disasters. "God it felt good to laugh like that. Been a while."

"That's what I'm here for—to provide you with comic relief about my horror show dating experiences when life gets you down."

Chuckling, Claire nudged her with her shoulder. "I appreciate the sacrifice. Where the hell do you meet these guys, anyway?"

Mel made a face, her nose wrinkling in distaste. "In all the wrong places, apparently."

"Oh no, that's all me," Zahra cut in. "And thus, I've sworn off dating for at least the next six months. I've decided to upgrade from my apartment, rent a house and adopt a bunch of rescue cats. If I can't find a decent man I want to be with, I can at least turn into a crazy cat lady in peace and quiet."

"You liar. I saw the way you and Dunphy were eyeing each other today when you thought no one was looking." Claire arched an eyebrow, daring her to deny it.

Zahra's dusky cheeks turned pink. "He's nice to look at. So what? Doesn't mean anything and I stand by my original claim. No men for the next six months. Just cats."

Mel shook her head in exasperation. "Zahra, I know I've just met you but I'm afraid I can't let you do that. A little self imposed celibacy is fine, but I draw the line at becoming a cat hoarder. You'll just have to hang out with Claire and me instead." Mel draped an arm around the taller woman's shoulders and started leading her toward her car. "Night, sweetie, drive safe," she called out to Claire. "And I want to hear every last detail about Gage next time we talk, or this friendship is over!"

"Nothing to tell," Claire called back, the mention of his name thankfully doing nothing to dampen her spirits. Man, a night out with the girls and a couple martinis and she felt like a new woman. After the nice relaxing glow from the drinks, they'd waited until the alcohol had worn off enough to allow her to drive home.

Out of habit she pulled out her phone to check for messages, then remembered the battery was dead. A blessing in disguise really, since now there'd be no texts asking her to stop by Danny's again before she headed home. Feeling relaxed and happy for once, she was looking forward to capping off her night curled up in bed with a good book.

Since it was almost nine, the traffic was light on the drive home and the rain had finally stopped. Turning onto her street she spotted her father's old pickup sitting in her driveway and let out a groan, the shine on her good mood slipping. She wasn't sure she had the mental energy to deal with any more family drama right now, and she damn sure didn't have any interest in doing so. Her father didn't come by often, not unless she invited him over for dinner or something, and she'd dropped off a load of groceries at his place only last night so she wasn't sure why he was here.

She parked next to his truck and grabbed her purse and laptop case from the passenger seat before climbing out of her vehicle. The front windows were lit up, telling her that her father was either in the kitchen or the family room. Maybe he'd stopped by to cook for her as a surprise? Not that she'd hold her breath on that one or anything.

The yard was in pretty sorry shape, she realized on her way to the front door, wishing she'd taken the time to clean up the leaves all over the lawn and driveway while they were dry instead of leaving them to get soaked and slimy. Now it'd be twice the work. When she unlocked the door and called for her father, the only warning she got that something was wrong was the absolute silence.

"Dad?" she called again, frowning as she set her laptop, keys and purse on the entry table by the door.

"In here, Claire."

At the sound of Gage's voice she froze, her heart stuttering. Immediately she whipped around to stare through the side panel window at the street. She'd been so distracted by the sight of her father's pickup in the driveway she'd failed to see Gage's vehicle parked at the curb across the street. What the hell was he doing here?

Already uneasy, she stepped around the corner of the entry wall and stopped dead at the sight before her. Her father and Gage both sat on her family room sofa, one on either end. Gage was leaning forward, forearms braced on his thighs, staring at her. Her father's eyes were red rimmed and bleary, his face blotchy. He'd been crying? She could count on one hand how many times she'd ever seen him cry. Fear snaked up her spine. There was only one reason she could think of for putting that look on her father's face and bringing the both of them here unannounced.

She felt brittle and exposed standing there, fear grinding in her gut.

"What—" Her throat closed up, suddenly too tight to get another word out. She swung her gaze to Gage. He stood and took a step toward her as though he intended to come to her, then stopped himself, his features set. Resigned.

"Come sit down, Claire." His voice was soft. Too soft, almost cajoling.

The fear turned into a full blown panic. Her heart slammed against her ribs. She shook her head and took an instinctive step back. She didn't want to sit down. Didn't want to hear what they were going to tell her. Denial and terror shot through her because deep down she already knew what they were going to say. "No." She shook her head and took another stumbling step back. "No, I don't want to hear it."

"Honey," her father rasped out, voice shot. His expression was filled with such anguish she knew her worst fears had just been confirmed.

Danny.

"No!" Before either of them could move she turned and bolted for the bathroom down the hall. Slamming the door shut behind her she locked it and leaned her back to it, clenching her hands in her hair, a wail of grief clawing its way up her throat. Her wobbling legs gave out and she slowly sank to the floor, caught between wanting to scream and the urge to crawl over to the toilet and throw up.

"Jesus, oh Jesus," she whimpered, rocking there on the cold tile floor with her arms wrapped around herself. She dimly realized she was shaking, hot tears rolling down her face. The horror and pain flooding her were too much. A hot pressure gripped her chest, squeezing the air from her lungs until it felt like her heart was about to implode. She fought to contain it, shove the agony away where it couldn't touch her but all that did was make her throat turn raw with the ugly, harsh sounds coming out of her. So many emotions crashed through her she couldn't process them all. Denial. Panic. Rage. And a deep, aching guilt that this was her fault.

"Claire." Gage's voice, steady and calm, just on the other side of the door. She hadn't heard him coming. "Claire, open the door."

No. She couldn't. Couldn't deal with this or having Gage see her at her most vulnerable. She curled into a tight ball and covered her head with her arms, wanting to scream. This had to be a bad dream. Any second now she'd wake up and everything would be okay again.

"Claire. Open it."

"N-no," she managed, gulping in ragged breaths in between the harsh sobs wracking her. She heard the sound of him settling against the door, heard his knees crack as he bent down.

Then, so gently she wept even harder, he kept talking to her. "Come out, sweetheart. You don't have to do this alone."

Claire curled up tighter and kept crying until she gagged. She lurched to her knees and lunged blindly for the toilet, got the seat up just in time. Her fingers curled around the edge of the plastic seat. As those first few terrible waves tore through her she dimly heard the sound of the lock rattling behind her. The door swung open a moment later. Still bent over the toilet bowl, she made a sound of misery and flung one hand out behind her to stave him off, humiliated and angry that he'd invade her privacy at a time like this. Then another wave seized her and she kept her head over the bowl as her stomach emptied itself with a gut-wrenching spasm.

Ignoring her wishes, Gage knelt beside her. One hand wrapped around the wad of hair she'd been trying to hold back while the other reached out to tear a strip of toilet paper from the holder on the wall beside the toilet. Between the vomiting and the crying she barely had enough control to suck in the occasional lungful of air, let alone have the strength to argue or fight him.

Her eyes watered too much for her to see what he was doing beside her. When nothing came up but bitter, acidic bile, her stomach eventually stopped rebelling and she weakly leaned her cheek against her forearms, braced on the toilet rim. Her eyes felt so swollen she could barely open them and she was shivering uncontrollably. Too weak to protest, she didn't resist when Gage raised her upper body to brace her against his chest. Automatically her hands came up to curl into the softness of his T-shirt and she hid her face there. This pain was unlike anything she'd ever experienced. She didn't know how she'd bear it.

Without a word Gage reached back to open the cabinet beneath the sink and took something out of it. He ran the tap for a second before shutting the water off and she heard him squeeze out a cloth in the sink. "Here," he said quietly, cupping the back of her neck to tip her head up enough for him to wipe her face.

She flinched at the cold of it, shocked back into a reality she had no desire to confront. Refusing to meet his eyes, she sat still and allowed him to wash all traces of tears and sickness from her face. He flushed the toilet, set the cloth in the sink and slipped his arms beneath her. "Come on." The powerful muscles in his arms and chest bunched beneath her hands and cheek as he hoisted her into the air and carried her out of the bathroom.

In the family room he eased her onto the loveseat across from the sofa and didn't protest when she turned away from him to curl into a ball at the arm of it. He placed the throw blanket over her but she didn't feel the warmth. Exhaustion and numbness were beginning to steal through her body and she welcomed them both.

"Wayne, would you mind getting her a drink? She'll have orange juice in the fridge."

"Sure." Her father pushed to his feet and shuffled into the kitchen, leaving her with the last person on earth she could afford to be alone with at the moment. He'd even remembered she always kept orange juice on hand—the pure stuff, not the concentrated crap. Every morning after he'd spent the night at her place they'd sat either at the kitchen table or out on the back deck, drinking a glass of it with their breakfast. The reminder sent a fresh flood of tears to her already burning eyes.

Rather than try to hold her again Gage sank onto the loveseat beside her and this time kept his distance. Not an easy thing to do considering how small the piece of furniture was and how much space his solid frame took up. Claire kept her eyes closed, not wanting to look at him or her father. It was all she could do to breathe with this invisible vise crushing her chest.

The familiar scent of her father's aftershave reached her a moment later, then he set a glass on the table beside her with quiet click that told her he'd remembered to use one of the coasters she kept there. She swallowed the hard lump in her throat and took a deep, steadying breath before prying her eyes open to face him across the room where he'd sat back on the sofa.

"When?" she asked, her throat so raw it came out a croak.

Her father's stubbled jaw quivered a second, then firmed before he answered. "They think sometime early this morning."

He'd been gone that long, lying there alone and undiscovered? "Did he overdose?"

Instead of answering her he shot a questioning look at Gage, and her stomach twisted again as he turned his eyes back on her. "No. Guess he wanted to make sure this time, so…" He clamped his lips together and sucked in a shuddering breath through his nose. When he had control of himself he continued. "He put his service pistol in his mouth and pulled the trigger."

Her stomach turned. She closed her eyes and turned away, unable to cope with it. Except all she saw now on the backs of her closed lids was the image of her brother's brain matter sprayed all over the walls of his cluttered apartment. She gagged, bolted into a sitting position.

Gage reached for her but she held him off with a mute shake of her head and swallowed repeatedly. The shivers were still coursing through her, convulsive shudders that hurt her muscles. It took more than a minute of focused breathing before she could trust herself not to throw up again. She settled back into the corner of the loveseat and looked over at her father. "Did the police call you?"

"They came to my house around four this afternoon. I called your cell right away and kept trying but I couldn't get through, then I tried you at work but only got your voicemail."

"I was in meetings all afternoon and my cell's dead." And after that she'd been out sharing drinks and laughs with Mel and Zahra, while her brother was lying dead in his apartment and her father had been frantically trying to reach her.

"I didn't know how else to get in touch with you so I came over and found Gage's number. I asked him to be here when you got back because I thought it might...make things easier for you."

She understood that he thought he'd been doing her a favor. He didn't realize that having Gage here was only making her bleed more inside, like dying a slow death from a thousand cuts. "Was there a note?"

Again he hesitated before answering and she felt her body tense in reaction, as though it expected a physical blow. "Yeah. I told the police to keep it because it was stained with...his blood and I couldn't handle seeing it." A glaze of tears turned his eyes glassy. "It said, 'I'm sorry, I can't handle this anymore. Please forgive me. Your lives will be better without me here. Love you both.' That was all."

The leaden weight in her chest cavity seemed to be spreading, filling her abdomen and creeping down her limbs. A high-pitched ringing started up in her ears and the room tilted. She shot out a hand to steady herself against the arm of the loveseat.

Gage reached past her, picked up the juice and held the glass to her lips. "Take a sip."

She started to shake her head but thought better of it and did as he said, hating that he was here to witness this drama and see her at her absolute worst. His acceptance and caring were unbearable right now.

The sweet/tart juice hit her parched tongue, flooded her mouth with saliva. She had to swallow twice to get each sip down, but the sugar hit her system fast and the worst of the wooziness passed. When she was half finished with the juice she gently pushed Gage's hand away and he set the glass back on the coaster.

"I called your mother," her father announced, making Claire look up at him in astonishment. It was no secret that they didn't communicate at all, and hadn't since she remarried. He shrugged. "Figured she should hear it from me. She's flying in day after tomorrow. Danny's at the hospital now but they're releasing him to the funeral home tomorrow. I'm not sure I… Do you want to see him?"

The thought of seeing her brother's body, knowing part of his skull was blown out filled her with revulsion. "No. God, no. And he wouldn't want any of us seeing him like that either."

Her father nodded, no judgement in his gaze. "I think he'd want a quiet service."

"Just family," she confirmed. Danny would've hated a giant spectacle on his behalf. "I'll take care of the arrangements first thing in the morning." The words were so surreal it was hard to believe they'd come out of her mouth.

His shoulders, always so broad and strong to her, suddenly seemed thin and frail as he sagged a little. "Thanks. I don't think I could handle that. And I know things have been really hard on you since Danny was wounded. You've been amazing through everything." He paused, gave a bitter laugh. "Hell, ever since your mother walked out." He placed his palms on his thighs and straightened, looked her square in the eye. "I want you to know how much I appreciate everything you've done for me and Danny over the years."

It hadn't been enough though. Her throat tightened. Such a simple declaration, but it made her want to cry all over again. "You're welcome." She'd hated watching them destroy themselves. She hated losing Danny more.

Those callused, work-worn hands rubbed up and down over his faded jeans, betraying his inner turmoil. "We have to remember Danny as he used to be," he said, voice wobbling with the effort of keeping his grief in check. "He'd want that. We have to remember that he was sick, that there was nothing any of us could do to make him want to stay here."

She'd told herself that same thing more times than she could count over the past two years, but she'd also never stopped hoping that he'd come back to them one day. Snap out of the funk he'd sunk into and see how many things he had left to be thankful for, all the reasons he had to live for. The throbbing in her temples suddenly intensified with a vengeance. She rubbed circles there with her fingertips, still struggling to accept that this was reality and not just another nightmare.

Gage stood and left the room. She and her father were still sitting there in silence when he returned with some aspirin and placed them in her hand. His thoughtfulness sent an arrow of pain through her. She knew if she reached for him right now he'd wrap those strong arms around her and hold her for as long as she needed him to. And even though she was hurting unbearably, that would be cruel to them both.

With a murmured thanks she took the tablets and set about discussing funeral plans with her father.

He left her with a giant hug at ten o'clock and let himself out. Gage, however, seemed to have no intention of leaving. Something that simultaneously flooded her with relief and dread. He rose and picked up her empty glass from the end table beside her. "Want more? Something to eat?"

"Thanks, but I'm not hungry." All she felt right now was exhaustion. She pushed to her feet and followed Gage into the bright white country kitchen as he rinsed the glass and put it in her dishwasher. Still appearing at home here in spite of what she'd put him through. She searched for something to say. "I appreciate you coming over. That meant a lot to my dad, not having to break the news to me alone."

"I didn't do it for him."

She lowered her eyes and nodded once. "I know. Thank you."

He leaned back against the granite counter, hands braced on the edge on either side of him. "No problem." He stared at her, a shadow of hurt in his eyes. *It didn't mean a lot to you?* they demanded silently.

Yes it meant a lot to her and he knew it, but he also knew why she wasn't going to say it. She was already having trouble remembering why she shouldn't just step into those strong arms and hide for a while, let him chase the worst of this stark anguish and guilt away. He was making it near impossible for her to stay detached from him. She cleared her throat, glanced away to the neatly arranged stacks of cream-ware dishes nestled in the glass-front cabinets above the L-shaped counter. "God, I'm wiped. I need to go to bed."

"Sure, go ahead." He made no move to leave.

Not liking what that meant, she tried a different tack. "I won't be in to work tomorrow, and maybe not for the rest of the week, so I'm not sure when I'll talk to you again." Despite the dismissal she meant it as, the thought of not seeing him filled her with a terrible hollowness.

Still calm, he raised one auburn eyebrow in defiance. "You're not staying here by yourself tonight."

She should have expected this. "I'm okay."

"No, you're not, and it pisses me off that you'd even pull that shit with me." He dragged a hand over his skull trim in exasperation, giving her an eyeful of bulging biceps. "Look, whatever shit that's gone down between us in the past, this supersedes all of it. I don't want you to be alone right now, so I'm staying. End of story."

She shook her head, feeling her control slip. "Gage, I can't handle this right now," she blurted, the hot pressure of tears flooding her throat. "I *can't...*"

With a low curse he closed the distance between them, ignoring her feeble protests as he gathered her up in his arms. She should have pushed away, said something nasty to make him leave but she couldn't bring herself to do it. It would have made her feel even worse and he didn't deserve it. Her body and heart didn't care that her brain was screaming at her that she was an idiot. They craved him, only him, and weren't letting her walk away.

Instead she wound her arms around his sturdy neck and buried her nose in the center of his wide chest, breathing in his familiar, comforting scent. He was right; in spite of all the damage she'd done to their relationship in the past, Danny's suicide had turned her world upside down. She needed Gage and didn't want him to go, not after all these lonely months spent aching for the chance to feel this again.

Those warm, strong hands stroked up and down her shuddering back as he crooned reassurances into the hair at her temple. She squeezed her eyes shut, throat constricting as she thought of how many nights she'd lain awake yearning for the feel of his body up against hers like this.

"I'm here for you, no matter what," he was saying softly, his warm breath brushing over her damp cheek. "I swear I'm not gonna push you for anything else, okay? Just let me stay."

Unable to speak, afraid that she'd blurt out her feelings for him, that she'd made a horrible mistake by walking away from him all those months ago, she nodded.

"Come on." He gently eased her away and steered her into her bedroom. Leaving her only for a moment to turn back the quilt on her queen-size four poster bed, he turned back and held out a hand. "Strip down to your undies and get in."

The idea of stripping down to *anything* in front of him probably wasn't the best idea but she was too tired to care and was just grateful he was staying. Unbuttoning her blouse and skirt, she peeled them off and flung them over a chair in the corner to deal with in the morning. She was already dreading waking up and facing what the day would bring.

Acutely aware of the way Gage's gaze swept over her body and lingered on the black lace bra and thong she wore, she averted her eyes and stepped past him to climb between the sheets he held back. Weariness engulfed her the moment she laid her head on the pillow. Gage pulled the covers up and tucked them beneath her chin, paused to stroke a comforting hand over her head, smoothing her hair back from her face.

"Get some sleep," he whispered. "I'll be here when you wake up and help you with everything."

She nodded, was about to say something else when he straightened and stepped back. Something akin to panic lit up in her chest. Without thinking she shot out a hand and grabbed his thick wrist. He stopped, peered down at her questioningly. Claire struggled past the uncertainty and whispered, "Stay with me?"

The set of his shoulders eased and she thought she saw a flash of tenderness in his eyes. "Sure. Scoot over."

Not giving herself time to question her actions, Claire turned onto her side and moved to the far right side of the bed. A puff of cool air hit her skin as the covers lifted. The mattress dipped a moment later and then Gage's warmth settled against her back and hips. He tucked her into the curve of his much taller body and wrapped a protective arm around her waist.

"Thanks," she whispered hesitantly into the silence, aware of every single inch of contact and the low voltage hum running through her nerve endings.

The ghost of a kiss caressed the top of her head. "Shhh. Just go to sleep."

With a weary sigh she snuggled deeper into his embrace and let herself drift until the blackness of sleep overcame her.

CHAPTER SIX

Claire rolled over and opened her eyes the next morning, for a moment confused by the rumpled state of the other side of the bed. Then it hit her all over again. Grief and shock that Danny was gone, the reality that it was really happening. She curled into a ball and focused on taking slow, deep breaths until the worst of the pain eased enough to allow her lungs to expand.

A clinking sound came from the kitchen. She burrowed deeper beneath her quilt and blinked back the sheen of tears, placing her hand on the indent Gage's head had left in the other pillow. Twice she'd woken during the night and both times he'd tucked her back against his body without a word and stroked her hair until she fell asleep again.

How was she supposed to keep her distance from him now? During their entire relationship she'd never seen this gentle caretaker side of him. With his daughter, sure, but that was different. With Claire he'd always been strong and take-charge, had always lit her body up with effortless ease. Things between them had been intense and very physical, right from the start. The tenderness he'd shown her yesterday was devastating because she had no defense against it.

I don't know if I can get through this, she thought miserably, scrubbing a hand over her face.

She needed a shower to clear her head before walking out of this room to face him and the long list of unhappy tasks she had to complete. It was already almost nine o'clock. Dragging herself out of bed, she started the shower and stepped under the hot spray, letting the water soothe some of the stiffness out of her neck and shoulders. The thought of everything she had to deal with today, including her mother's impending arrival, made her long to crawl back into bed and pull the covers over her head. But she didn't cave under pressure, and she'd damn well face everything and anything she had to in order to see to Danny's final arrangements properly.

After brushing her teeth, blow-drying her hair and putting some makeup on her puffy eyes, she dressed in jeans and a lightweight pink sweater before heading into the kitchen. Gage wasn't there. She stopped in the doorway, her heart sinking. He'd up and left, just like that? She wasn't sure if that offended or crushed her.

A full pot of Italian roast waited for her on the counter though, along with her favorite mug and the carton of half and half from the fridge, remembering how she took her coffee. She was so confused about everything she didn't know *what* to think. Had he stayed last night out of a sense of compassion, or had it been obligation? Both those options sucked, and yet he'd given no indication that he wanted anything beyond the chance to help dull the worst of her grief. For that, she was grateful. And more disappointed than she could say.

Alone at the granite-topped island she sipped the coffee, a bittersweet rise of emotion filling her when she tasted how strong it was. Gage had always made it like that, no matter how much she'd argued with him about it. Funny how the little things triggered the most vivid memories after someone was gone.

The drone of a lawnmower started up outside, startling her. Claire turned toward the French doors that led out to the back deck and set her mug down just in time to see Gage stride by, pushing her mower. For a moment she was too stunned to move. The man was cutting her freaking lawn for her, a true old-fashioned Southern boy to his core.

Smiling a little, she carried her coffee over to the doors and watched him. Weak sunlight peeked through the sullen blanket of clouds. She admired the flex of muscle beneath the T-shirt stretched across his back and shoulders, the way his jeans hugged his ass and thighs. Gage at rest was a beautiful thing. In motion, he was a sight to behold.

She sighed, feeling her emotional walls crumble a bit more. Did she have the strength to deal with this on top of everything else? She'd been a complete and utter idiot to ever think she could live without this man. All her reasons for ending things with him, reasons she'd been convinced would mean certain doom for them if they'd stayed together, seemed so fucking stupid now. Especially today, when facing the reality of how quickly life could change.

Turning away from the doors she sat back at the island and with the sound of the mower as background music, pulled out a pen and paper to make a list of everything she needed to do. She was on the phone to a local funeral home when Gage came back inside from the front yard through the garage. She tensed, her instinctive reaction to ignore him, but what the hell good would that do at this point? It would only confirm she was the coward he'd accused her of being when she'd broken up with him.

Claire might be a lot of things, but a coward wasn't one of them.

Pushing aside her fear of rejection, she made herself turn on the barstool and offer him a smile to show him how grateful she was for the lawn, and that he'd stayed. He paused in surprise for a beat, hand poised to grab his own mug from the cupboard. Then he smiled back and turned away to reach inside the cupboard.

Some of the anxiety in her gut eased and it seemed a little easier to breathe all of a sudden. She wrote notes about what the funeral home director said and answered the more difficult questions about Danny's death. "He's still at the hospital. I've spoken to my parents, and we've decided not to have a viewing. He wanted to be cremated, so…" God, maybe it wasn't easier to breathe. She pressed a hand to her stomach, took a shuddering breath. "We'd like that taken care of as soon as possible," she finished in a rush.

"I understand," the director said in a soothing tone. "All we need you to do is come in and sign the paperwork. We'll handle everything else from there."

"I'd appreciate that." Once the call ended she set the phone down on the island and let out a long exhale. Gage chose a stool across from her and slid onto it.

"That the funeral home?" he asked, those endlessly blue eyes delving into hers. Assessing, measuring.

She nodded, wanting to show him her inner strength. "They need me to sign the paperwork to get everything in motion. I told him I'd head over right now."

"I'll drive you," he said, already pushing to his feet, mug in hand. "Just let me grab a quick shower."

"Gage."

He stopped and looked down at her, his expression inscrutable even though she knew he expected her to argue.

"Thank you," she said instead. "For last night, for the lawn and everything else."

The surprise evaporated, replaced by a spark of annoyance burning in his eyes. "Quit thanking me for every little thing. It's startin' to piss me off."

She blinked, taken aback by the unexpected response. "Okay. Just wanted you to know I appreciate what you've done."

"Yeah, got it. Give me five minutes." He stalked from the kitchen, leaving her wondering what invisible land mine she'd accidentally triggered. Blowing out a breath, she waited until he came back downstairs then grabbed her purse and followed him out to his SUV.

Despite the lingering strain between them, Gage drove her to the funeral home and offered to come in with her. She politely turned him down, needing to do this on her own without an audience, even him. When she came back to the truck an hour later she was on the verge of tears. In a few hours the funeral home would take Danny from the hospital morgue and bring him back here to be placed in an oven for cremation. Her hand shook when she reached for the door handle, a low grade nausea churning in her stomach.

Gage reached over and popped the door open for her, his other hand holding his phone to his ear as he met Claire's eyes and spoke to whoever was on the other end. "Hang on a sec, baby girl."

Claire knew from that endearment that he was talking to Janelle. He sat upright as she climbed in and shut the door, that perceptive gaze sweeping over her face, not missing the tears blurring her vision.

"I gotta go, sweetheart. Yeah, she's back now, but it's not a great time for you to talk to her. Maybe later, okay?" He paused, listening to whatever Janelle was saying. "I'll tell her.

Love you too. Bye." He set the phone down into the tray in the center console between them and met her gaze. "That was Janelle. I told her about Danny. She said to tell you she's sorry and to give you a big hug. She's gonna say a special prayer for him and your family at church tomorrow."

For some reason, that snapped the final threads holding together what was left of her frayed control. Claire covered her face with her hands and shuddered with the force of the sob locked in her throat. It didn't make any sense, but receiving that message of sympathy from a teenager was irrefutable evidence that Danny was gone forever.

Gage cursed softly and unbuckled his seat belt. "Ah hell, I'm sorry. C'mere."

She shook her head and turned toward the door to hide, hating that he was seeing her lose it like this yet again. He ignored her, leaning across the center console to draw her into a hug made even more awkward by the positioning. The moment her cheek touched his shirt she stopped resisting and leaned against him, thankful for the opportunity to bury her face into his chest. It took a while for her to regain her composure enough to pull away and wipe at her wet face.

"I got mascara on your shirt," she whispered unevenly, automatically reaching out to rub at the marks she'd left.

Gage gently pushed her hands away. "I don't give a fuck about my shirt," he told her, taking her chin in one hand to tip her face up. "Talk to me. What do you want to do now?"

She wasn't sure. Any denial phase she'd been experiencing was blown to hell at this point. Now she was starting to get mad. She welcomed it. "You know what? I'm pissed off."

He released her chin abruptly and leaned back in his seat to blink at her.

She let out a watery laugh at the stunned look on his face. "Not at you. At Danny." She shook her head, letting the anger roll through her. It felt good. Hell of a lot better than the hollow helplessness she'd woken up with. "He's threatened us with this for such a long time, it was always hanging over our heads. He'd veer from being nasty and bitter to yelling and swearing at us when we tried to help, then all of a sudden drop off the radar and not talk to anyone for days while he holed up with his stupid fucking pills and cases of beer. We walked on eggshells around him forever to avoid pushing him over the edge, and for what? He went and did it anyhow." She shook her head in frustration. "It was fucking selfish of him to take his life, and he knew it. God *damn* him for doing this."

Gage didn't say anything, but he seemed a bit taken aback by her rant.

"Seriously," she went on, wanting him to validate her. "You went through multiple combat tours and other stuff, and I know you saw and did awful things. Every vet comes home with shit to deal with, I get that." She could see examples of it right now, two of his soldiers' names lost in combat inked into the designs on the backs of his forearms beneath the sprinkling of reddish hair there. Yet he'd found the will to deal with it all on his own, where Danny had not no matter how she or her father and everyone involved with his case had pushed him.

She didn't understand why her brother had to wind up a statistic. "You came through the other side and transitioned back into civilian life. It's not like I blame him for being depressed and disillusioned, especially after his back injury, but I'm so fucking *angry* at him for quitting." That was the crux of it. He'd given up and his last act on earth was to do the one thing guaranteed to hurt the people who loved him the most. His suffering was over, but theirs had just begun.

Gage was silent a moment, and when he finally spoke his voice was low and quiet. "He didn't see any other way out, Claire. He didn't have any more fight left in him."

The matter-of-fact way he said it took the scorching edge off her temper as effectively as a bucket of ice water dumped over her head. Deflated, she closed her eyes and laid her head back on the seat with a sigh. "I know, but I'm still mad at him. Part of me wishes he was still here so I could shake him." But Danny had probably known that. He'd made it very clear he knew what a disappointment and burden he'd become to her and their father.

She ran a hand over her face, stared through the windshield without really seeing anything. "I know I'm at least a little to blame in all this."

"Don't say that."

"No, it's true. I made no secret about what I thought of his behavior, especially toward the end. And you know what the worst part is? There were many days when I wished he'd do it. Just fucking do it and get it over with so the rest of us could move on with our lives." She let out a bitter laugh, shook her head at herself in disgust. "Careful what you wish for, Claire. God, what kind of person thinks that about their own brother?"

"Stop beating yourself up. You went through your own hell with all this for the past two years. Everyone's got their limit. You're human, and that means you're not perfect and never will be. None of us are."

She turned her head to look at him, guilt an oily film coating her insides. "Do you think he knew I was thinking it?"

"Doesn't matter whether he did or not. Taking his life was his choice to make and no one else's. Maybe that's why he did it. It was the only control he felt he had left over anything."

Yes, she could see Danny thinking that, and it made her feel sick. Needing the connection, she reached out and took Gage's hand, laced her fingers through his and squeezed. "I'm so glad you never gave up when things got hard."

It wasn't meant as a double entendre about their relationship as well, but maybe that was a subconscious slip on her part. Gage nodded once, squeezed her hand in return and didn't let go. "Me too. Still have my moments though. PTSD is such a piss poor term because it means a million different things to a million different people and everyone's experience of it is unique. What we see and do in the line of duty, it leaves a mark. It did on me. I don't think it'll ever go away completely and in a way I don't want it to. Good and bad, what I've been through helped shape me into who I am today."

"You mean a former master sergeant with a foul mouth and a habit of ordering everyone around?" she teased.

The corner of his mouth tipped upward in a self-deprecating grin. "Yeah, that too." Slowly, as though he had to force himself to do it, he pulled his hand free from hers and turned the key in the ignition. "So, where to now?"

She folded her hands in her lap and chided herself for being disappointed that he'd severed the physical contact. What did she expect when nothing was resolved between them? She definitely didn't have the energy for that conversation right now, nor did she want to go to Danny's place yet. "To my dad's, I guess. But look, if you've got things to do with the team, I totally understand. Just take me home and I'll drive there myself."

He cut her a sharp look and she fought back a smile at the outrage on his face before he spoke. "I told Tom and Hunter I needed a few days off unless something important comes up where they need me. If they do, they'll call. If not, I'm staying with you."

"Okay." She stopped herself from saying thanks just in time, remembering how annoyed he'd been with her for that earlier.

He not only took her to her dad's and helped them go through all the legal paperwork, he stayed through an incredibly awkward lunch when her mother and stepfather came over. The whole time he stayed at her side but didn't touch her, a steady, solid presence while they discussed and finalized funeral arrangements. They all wanted it over and done with as quickly as possible, and managed to organize everything for the following afternoon. Claire would host the reception after the short memorial service at the funeral home chapel. Her mother felt strongly about inviting some friends and other relatives, so she and her father gave in and started making calls.

Claire studied her mother while she was on the phone to some acquaintance or another. For the most part they'd patched up their relationship since Claire had become an adult, so they were on much better terms than they had been while she was growing up. Since the divorce her mother had been so preoccupied with her new husband and babies, she'd only kept in touch with Claire through phone calls and the occasional visit, which Claire had hated initially because it felt like her half-siblings had stolen her mother from her. The woman hadn't been there for Danny since the day she'd walked out of their lives, and part of Claire resented her for being here now. She tried to reason with herself that no matter how things had deteriorated between them over the years, Danny had been her first child. It didn't help. Her mother showing up and taking over today didn't magically erase everything she'd put them all through.

Toward dinnertime everything caught up with her and Claire started to fade. Her mother was going on about what kind of flowers to order for the service and what sort of sandwiches to have at the reception, and Claire couldn't care less. "Whatever you want, mom. Let's just get this done so we can go home and get some sleep. Tomorrow's gonna be a tough day." She was dreading it already. It was all too fresh, she wasn't ready to say goodbye to Danny forever.

She was sitting on her father's front room couch with Gage when she gave up trying to stifle her yawns. Without a word he draped a heavy arm around her shoulders and tugged her close. She sighed at the feel of those warm, solid muscles bracing her. Within seconds of resting her head on his shoulder, she was asleep. The next thing she knew, he was urging her upright.

"What time is it?" she blurted, glancing around. Her mother and stepfather were gone, so it was just her, Gage and her father. The TV was on, an action flick they'd all seen before.

"Just after eight," Gage answered. "Let's get you home." He pulled her to her feet and she didn't protest. Once in the truck, instead of taking her home he drove to her favorite takeout place and paid for their dinner. They ate together at her kitchen table in an easy silence. When everything was cleaned up and there were no more arrangements to be taken care of she wasn't sure what to do with herself, but she knew she didn't want to be alone yet.

"Want to watch a movie or something?" she asked him.

He shook his head. "You're dead on your feet. Go on to bed."

A taut silence stretched out between them and she didn't know how to fill it. Did she invite him to her bed again? Because she knew she'd never be able to keep her hands off him, exhausted or not, and there was always the chance he'd reject her outright if she touched him.

She cleared her throat. "Do you—"

"I'll take the couch."

She hid a flinch at the finality in his tone. "Sure. I'll grab you some blankets." Going to the linen closet upstairs gave her a minute alone to think. She couldn't read him. Had no idea what was going on in his head. Very unlike Gage, who'd always been so open with her.

If she'd lost him for good, it was her own damn fault, she thought angrily. A different kind of grief seeped into her, leaving her cold and empty.

Carrying a pillow and some blankets, she made her way downstairs to find that he'd already pulled the back cushions off the couch. It was long enough to fit his tall frame if he curled up a bit, and without the back cushions he'd have plenty of room. She wished she had an extra bed to offer him but she'd turned the guestroom into an office when she'd moved in. She didn't bother offering him her room because she knew he'd turn her down flat and get irritated with her all over again.

Gage took the pillow. "Thanks." He dropped it at one end of the couch and reached back for the first blanket. Hating the distance between them, she helped him tuck it into the frame like a fitted sheet and shook out the heavy quilt he'd use as a blanket. When it was done he looked over at her, poised at the other end of the couch, as if he wasn't sure why she was still standing there, and stared. Swallowing, she shifted from one foot to the other. Did she lay it all out on the line here and now?

"Not tired anymore?" he guessed.

"No, I'm completely beat."

"Go ahead and get to bed then. I'm good. See you in the morning."

The dismissal registered but she couldn't make herself leave. Something warned her that if she didn't do something to close this emotional divide she'd be sorry, and regret it for the rest of her life.

He was still standing there, unmoving, watching her with an unreadable expression. With the kitchen light still on there was enough light for her to see the wariness in his eyes. She hated that look. Hated it more that she'd put it there. More than ever she realized how much she needed him. And so far he'd been there for her every step of this hellish journey. He was the kind of man she could depend on for anything and she wanted him beside her from this moment on.

He didn't want her thanks and she didn't know what else to say. But sometimes action was better than words.

Before she could change her mind, she took two steps to close the distance between them, reached up to take his face in her hands and leaned up to kiss him.

Huge mistake.

He made a low sound and slanted his mouth over hers. Sexual need slammed into her. It hit her like a blast wave, so strong it made her shudder. His taste. God, she'd forgotten how good he tasted, how soft his lips were.

She crowded in closer with an inarticulate sound and plastered her body against his muscular frame, desperate for more. Gage growled low in his throat and slid his hands into her hair, his tongue eagerly exploring her mouth. Her nipples tightened, breasts swelling as tingles raced along her nerve endings, centering in the throbbing pulse in her core. He was all hard, taut muscle, his body all but vibrating with unrelieved tension. Claire surrendered to the lust driving her and kissed him harder, demanding everything he had to give.

It was always like this with him. Zero to ninety in the space of a heartbeat. She was melting, liquid heat pooling low in her belly and between her thighs. She wanted him to throw her onto that couch and blanket her with his weight, fill her completely and pound into her until she came so hard she screamed his name. When it came to making her scream in ecstasy, Gage was an expert.

Her throaty, needy moan drifted into the air between them, charging the room with electricity. His hands locked her head in place as he crushed his mouth down over hers, the steely length of his erection pressed against her lower abdomen. She was drowning, already slipping under the dark waves of desire when he suddenly ripped his mouth away from her and released her head.

Gasping, Claire reached for his shoulders to steady herself. He caught her upper arms but as soon as she'd straightened he released her and stepped back. She licked her lips, stared at him. He was breathing roughly, his stare hot enough to melt metal. He wanted her, every bit as badly as she did him. "What—"

He shook his head sharply. "Bad idea."

Her heart constricted. "I—" *Want you. I need you. I never stopped loving you.* But she couldn't force the words out. They made her feel too vulnerable in the face of his rejection.

Gage blew out a frustrated breath and scrubbed a hand over his face, clearly fighting for control. "God, just… Look, you're going through a lot and I understand why you want this right now but I'll be damned if I'm gonna be something you regret tomorrow morning when you're thinking clearly again." She opened her mouth to protest and tell him she *was* thinking clearly but he talked right over her. "Let's just get through the next couple days and once everything's settled down we'll talk about us then, okay?"

The vise-like pressure around her heart eased somewhat. Her body was crying out for him, though not just for the physical release he offered but dammit, she knew he was right. Things were still way too unsettled between them to throw sex into the mix. Even if it would've been mind-blowing, nuclear meltdown sex that left them both sweaty and too exhausted to move until morning.

"Okay," she made herself whisper, telling herself there was still hope for more if he'd promised to talk later. Gage always kept his promises. "Sleep well."

"You too."

Yearning for him more with every step, she forced her feet to carry her upstairs to her empty bed and shut the door behind her.

CHAPTER SEVEN

C ome *on*, did these people never leave their damn
house on the weekend?

Mo fumed silently as he drove past for the second time that day and saw two SUVs still in the driveway.
And now the damn lawn was already cut, too, which totally
blew his cover and plans to hell. He hit the gas and continued
down the street, searching for another option. Nothing came
to mind, except for a direct assault on the house and he'd
prefer not to die in this operation. His dedication didn't
extend all the way to suicide to ensure the target was eliminat-
ed. What the hell was he supposed to do now?

Halfway down the block, his cell rang. A burner phone
he'd picked up the day before at the local mall. He knew who
it was without looking, contemplated not answering, but knew
he'd be in even greater danger if he ignored it. Pulling over, he
tamped down the fear and frustration twining through him
and answered. "Hello?"

"We've had no word from you in two days. Is there a
problem?" Urdu. Which meant the man on the other end
wasn't worried about anyone eavesdropping on the call. Mo
was glad at least one of them felt confident about that.

He set his jaw before answering. "The target is proving difficult to isolate." And now he couldn't even use the identity of a landscaper as an excuse to get the job done. He'd called a landscaper friend to borrow his truck under the guise of having to pick up a new couch. Now all the truck did was make him run the risk of being conspicuous.

"Why do you need to isolate them? We told you to take care of this by any means necessary. Perhaps you misunderstood our meaning?"

Mo gritted his teeth. "I understand what you want. I'll get it done."

"You will have until Tuesday evening to complete your task, and then we will be forced to take other measures."

The line went dead before he could respond, but really, what was there to say? Frustrated, he threw the phone across the bench seat. It hit the door and fell to the passenger floorboard with a thud as he put the vehicle into drive.

He kept driving until he was out of the residential neighborhood and making his way north back to the city center. Mo knew all too well what those *other measures* were and he wanted no part of them. But damn, he'd wanted to make this as clean as possible, walk away and be long gone when the explosion happened. Looked like that might not be an option anymore.

Cold, clammy sweat broke out across his face and chest, under his arms. His shirt was already sticking to his skin and the conversation had only ended two minutes ago. There was no way he'd be able to sleep tonight. He had to fix this, find another way. He was smart and motivated, even more so with that subtle threat against his life the man had just made.

A horn blared. He blinked and jerked the wheel to the left just in time to avoid crashing into a minivan that had turned the corner. Damn he hadn't even seen it, hadn't even realized he'd run a red light. The driver, a woman ferrying around a load of elementary aged kids, was glaring daggers at him and shouting something he didn't catch. Mo quickly merged into the other lane and turned onto a different street, deciding to take an alternate route home. The fewer people who saw him, the safer he'd be.

He had to regroup and figure out what the hell to do, and fast. Because if he wanted to live through this, he had to kill the target well before the Tuesday night deadline.

Sean Dunphy backed the SUV he and Ellis were sharing out of the driveway, careful not to knock over the bags of grass clippings he'd set there an hour ago, and drove down the street. The neighborhood was quiet this Sunday morning, only a few people out working in their yards to take advantage of the break in the weather.

The sky was overcast and promising more rain, but for now the roads were dry. Even though he was going to a funeral later, the day was looking up for him. Because in a few minutes he'd be picking up Zahra and have her all to himself until the service. And, if things went well, hopefully afterward too. Maybe until they both had to climb out of the tangled bed sheets to get to work the next morning.

He pulled out to pass a truck with a lawnmower in the back that suddenly pulled over to the curb without signalling. His mood was so good he didn't even bother glaring at the driver on the way past. Traffic was light and he made the drive to Zahra's apartment building in less than fifteen minutes. He parked out front and was just getting out of the vehicle when she stepped out of the building's entrance.

The black knee length dress she wore was conservative, but on her it was a statement of sexy elegance. Her long wavy black hair was wound up into some sort of knot at the back of her head, which only emphasized her large hazel eyes and the sharp cut of her cheekbones. His gaze swept down the length of her, admiring the way that dress hugged her subtle curves, down to those sexy bare calves and black high heels. God help him, he had to get through a funeral with her looking like that, when all he wanted to do was look at her.

Realizing he was staring, he jerked his eyes back to her face and put on a friendly smile, trying not to gawk. "Hey, I was just going to text you."

"I saw you pull up," she answered, sliding her purse strap up higher on her toned shoulder and walking toward him with a confident stride that made him want to groan in appreciation. Today the slight hitch in her gait was almost invisible and he wondered why, and what had caused it. Most people wouldn't have noticed it in the first place, but then, most people weren't as observant as him. After spending the past few years serving with the best recon unit in the military, he'd learned to see things others didn't.

Zahra drew him in a way he didn't fully understand but he didn't care about the why of it. The woman was independent to the point of aloofness and moved with a regal grace that never failed to draw his eye. She stepped past him to the door he'd opened for her, slid inside with a murmur of thanks and a flash of dusky thigh as the hem of her dress rode up. Her scent drifted up to tease him, a mix of warm amber and even warmer woman that made the front of his pants incredibly tight all of a sudden. Sean shut the door behind her and hurried around the hood to get behind the wheel.

"Thanks for picking me up," she said as he steered away from her building, casting him a sidelong glance out of those amazing hazel eyes made even more vivid by the thick fringe of black lashes that surrounded them.

"No problem. Wish it could've been for a nicer reason though."

She turned her head to look out the windshield with a sigh. "Yeah. Poor Claire. How is she doing, have you heard?"

"Gage is with her. Says she's holding up well."

"She would. She's tough, but I guess that's to be expected when your brother and father were ex-Green Berets."

"Guess so."

"And speaking of ex-Green Berets, are she and Gage…back together?" she asked cautiously.

He glanced over, caught the slight frown wrinkling her brow. "No idea. Want me to call him up and ask him?"

She laughed softly and waved his offer away with a graceful flick of one hand. "No. Sorry, I can't help being nosy. It's in my nature."

Well, it was his nature to make people laugh and he loved the sound of hers. He wanted to hear it more often. "That's probably what makes you so good at your job. Your penchant for wanting to investigate."

"You mean my obsession? Yeah, probably. I've noticed you're pretty good with details yourself."

He just smiled and kept his eyes on the road. "I'd better be."

"You were a Recon Marine, right?"

He nodded. "For six years."

He had her full attention now. He could see her watching him curiously out of the corner of his eye. "Do you miss it?"

"Sometimes." He shrugged. Sure as hell didn't miss the conditions and lack of equipment they always seemed to suffer out in the field. "Mostly I just miss the guys."

"Why'd you get out?"

"It was time." Not wanting to talk about that anymore, he shifted the conversation to her. "What about you? You graduated from MIT, right?"

"I did."

"With honors."

"Also true," she said with a little smile. "Though I'll admit, I didn't realize the Marine Corps taught people such good computer skills. Might've rethought my decision and enlisted instead, if I'd known."

"Oh, you'd be surprised what skills I picked up during my time there."

"No, I don't think I would, actually." Still smiling, she folded her arms beneath her breasts, which of course made him steal another look there. She was trim and toned, but still soft in all the right places. And despite the conservative way she always dressed, she exuded an innate sensuality that tantalized him. It was damned distracting, considering they had to work together so closely. He'd been fantasizing about her since the first day they'd met.

He'd love to stop at the next light to lean across the console, watch those incredible eyes go wide as he bent and inhaled the fragrance of her skin just below her ear. His fingers itched to stroke across her smooth cheek and down her throat to her bare shoulder, slip beneath the neckline of that dress and find out what she was wearing beneath it. Because he'd bet every cent he owned that her bra was silky soft and just as sexy as she was.

Jerking his gaze back to the road, he tamped down his impatience at having to curb the impulse. If he rushed this she'd bolt. That was the last thing he wanted, and he wanted more than the one night stands he'd become so bored with. With Zahra he'd like the chance to get to know her on a personal level, see if things developed naturally from there.

"Hunter said you stayed late at work last night," he heard himself say. "Anything interesting turn up?"

Rather than answer right away, she shifted in her seat and pointedly avoided his gaze.

He looked back at her. He could read changing conditions on a battlefield in an instant, know exactly where and how to hit a target, but he could also read people just as well. She knew something and didn't want to tell him. "What? What did you find?"

She nibbled her plump lower lip for a second before responding. "I'm not really sure if it's anything. I called Alex last night to talk to him about it. He said he'd look into it further and let us know after the service today if he thinks it's worth all of us following up with."

Bullshit. She was damn good at her job and a hard worker. If she'd found something she thought was important enough to work half the night on and report her findings to Alex, then it was something they all needed to look at. "Zahra, what did you find?" he prompted, his body tensing slightly.

Her foot tapped on the floor mat. "I was translating some more of that chatter you and I found yesterday."

"From the satellite feed?"

She nodded, met his eyes at last. The serious expression on her face put him on instant alert. "Remember the lead we've been following from the chat room? Abdullo?"

"I remember." The guy was suspected to have ties with a militant network in Tajikistan, as well as being linked to the TTP. "What about him?"

"I was translating his phone transmissions. He's been very clever so far, only using the same phone a couple of times, but the voice recognition software matched him to this other conversation and I started listening in. It was to someone in Baltimore."

Sean processed all that in silence. "And?"

"It was a short conversation made a few days ago, and I wouldn't have paid much attention to it except that the man he called spoke in English rather than Urdu, and the entire conversation was cryptic. I think so he wouldn't raise suspicion if anyone else overheard. Abdullo said something about needing this guy's 'trusted services' and said there was an envelope waiting for him with all the necessary information. He was to call Abdullo back with his decision about taking the job."

Sounded like a terrorist cell activating a sleeper cell here in the States. "Did you trace this guy in Baltimore?"

"I looked him up, but couldn't find anything else that might link him to a terror network. He's not on any of the watch lists as far as I could tell and if he called Abdullo back I can't find a record of it, so maybe he used a different phone. And I couldn't find any record of Abdullo's incoming calls after. That's why I stayed so late—I thought I was close to finding all the pieces but I never did."

All his instincts were screaming that this bastard was planning some kind of attack in the area, and soon. Was it Claire? Hunter and the rest of the team had to know what was going on, and to hell with waiting on Alex and whoever else at the NSA was working this thing. He pulled his cell out of his pocket and hit a number before holding it out to her. "It's Hunt. Tell him everything, right now."

Zahra took it without arguing and relayed the information when Hunt picked up. Sean took a deep breath and drove to the funeral home, knowing that by the time they got there, Zahra's boss and half the NSA's counter-terrorist people would already be working on this. And he also knew that as soon as the funeral was over, the entire team would be pulling an all-nighter except for Claire and maybe Gage. And if Sean was in his place, he wouldn't let Claire out of his sight for a single second until they figured out if this bastard was the threat they'd been trying to neutralize.

By nine o'clock that night, Gage could tell Claire was done with pretty much everything. She was done with everything surrounding Danny's funeral, finished with her relatives, and hell, definitely finished with people in general. No surprise to him, because it had been a long, emotionally exhausting day for her.

The service had gone well enough, though there'd been way more people there than Claire and her father had wanted, thanks to her mother calling up all kinds of acquaintances after she and her husband had gone back to her hotel last night. That inconsiderate move had only caused Claire more stress as she'd been forced to run around buying more groceries this morning and then had spent all her time prior to the service prepping the food. Gage had helped out as much as he could, cleaning, chopping and assembling the stupid crustless tea sandwiches Claire's mother had insisted on. Didn't matter that the woman had come over to help, Gage was still pissed at her for putting more stress on Claire.

At the funeral Claire had insisted he sit with her in the front pew, with him and her father flanking her and Mel directly behind her. Claire had looked around at all the additional "mourners" and he'd seen the fury and disgust burning in her eyes. *Where the hell were they during the past two years?* she'd demanded in an angry whisper, her body vibrating with tension. *If they didn't care about Danny enough to be there for him when he was alive, then they have no right to be here now to stare at his urn.*

KAYLEA CROSS

He couldn't agree more. Unable to do anything to make it any easier on her, he'd sat with his arm around her while the minister had presided over the service and read the eulogy Claire had written for Danny, offering what comfort he could. She'd stayed quiet and strong throughout the service. Too strong. He knew how much she was hurting even if no one else could. The last thing he wanted was to see her break under the strain of it all. And now a lot of those same people who had filled the little chapel had come back to her place for the reception that had started well over four hours ago. With one look at her drawn face now, he knew she wanted everyone to take the hint and get the hell out. Trouble was, she was too polite a hostess to ever say it.

"Okay people, feel free to leave any time," Mel murmured as she stepped up beside him, wiping her hands on a dish towel. She'd been a godsend all day, doing whatever needed to be done without complaint. Of all Claire's friends, Mel was his favorite. "When do you think they'll take the hint and get out?" she whispered to him.

"When all the free food and booze is gone," Gage muttered darkly.

"I already shoved the last few platters into the back of the fridge so no one sees them, and I put away all the bottles that were on the counter. Want me to light something on fire to set off the smoke alarm?"

His lips quirked. "Might come to that. I'll give you the signal."

Mel sighed and leaned her head against his shoulder. Gage lifted his arm and draped it across her shoulders. "I'm really glad you're here," she told him quietly. "I sleep better knowing she's got you to look after her."

He'd do a hell of a lot more than look after her if she'd let him. "Thanks."

She tilted her head back to look at him. "It's good to have you back. I've missed you, you know."

"Missed you too, sweet pea." Too bad he wouldn't be around for very long. And probably less than that if Claire had her way. He was still sure he'd averted disaster last night by turning her down, even if he'd wanted her so much his hands had been shaking.

Mel blushed like she always did when he called her that, but he knew she liked it. Together they stood in the doorway and watched in silence as Claire played hostess. After a full minute, Mel eased away. "I can't take this anymore. I'll be in the kitchen, watching for the signal. Make sure it's noticeable."

"All right. Stand by."

Claire needed peace and quiet after everything she'd gone through today. He'd felt the same way every time he'd attended a buddy's funeral, and she'd just come from saying goodbye to her only sibling, the man she'd looked up to for most of her life.

He leaned against the kitchen wall, watching her move around the living room filling up glasses, handing out food, and generally worrying about shit she shouldn't have to. He had to keep reminding himself of the new foreign boundaries imposed upon him by their estrangement. Had it been six months ago he knew exactly how he would have handled things. Now he was forced to stand back and watch her drive herself into the ground right in front of him.

Another half hour passed and only one or two people trickled out. Claire was more than courteous to the few guests still hanging around, but he could read her better than anyone and so he knew she was hanging on to the last of her composure by a rapidly fraying thread. Her smile was forced, almost brittle, her movements short and jerky. The irritation in her eyes had long since turned to flat out annoyance and he knew it was only a matter of time before she exploded.

To save her from that embarrassment and not wanting Mel to actually set fire to anything, he decided to ignore the unspoken rules and take care of the situation himself.

Pushing away from the wall, he stepped into the center of the room and used his NCO voice, honed to perfection by more than seventeen years of service. "Thank you all for coming out to support Claire and her family today. We appreciate everyone being here, but it's been a long day and if ya'll don't mind we'd like to wrap this up now."

A shocked silence met his words, followed by an awkward hush. Claire's head snapped around, her eyes wide with incredulity before she narrowed them at him. He stared right back unapologetically and mentally raised a defiant eyebrow at her. She didn't like his methods? Too fucking bad. His only concern right now was her and he didn't give a shit what anyone else thought.

The guests all looked at him in surprise, including Claire's parents. Mel walked past him and started clearing up, and that seemed to make it official. After a heartbeat of awkward hesitation, everyone stood up and got moving. Some carried their cups and plates into the kitchen. Others went to Claire and her parents with a murmur of condolence and left, sliding him a sidelong glance as they walked out the door.

He hurried them along with a glacial look and a tight-lipped smile that barely passed for civil. It didn't take long for them to all clear out, five minutes tops. When only Mel, Claire's parents and stepfather remained, Wayne came up to Gage and clapped a hand on his shoulder.

"Sure glad to have you here with us today. And thanks for kicking everyone out. I wanted to in the worst way." He nodded toward Claire, who was in the kitchen with her mother and stepfather and Mel, cleaning up. "I think in a lot of ways this whole thing is hardest on her. She needs some time alone."

Gage nodded, not bothering to disagree. Although being alone wasn't going to be an option for her tonight, and not for the next few nights at least if he had anything to say about it. "Do you need a ride home?"

Wayne gave a sad, weary smile that reminded Gage too much of Danny, but at least he wasn't drunk. He broke eye contact before answering. "I only had three beers, I'm good." He shoved his hands into his pockets, cleared his throat as he looked around Claire's living room and shook his head. "Helluva thing, isn't it? I always thought I'd be the one to eat a bullet instead of Danny."

Not what Gage wanted to hear. He waited for the older man to look at him again and pinned Wayne's gaze with his own. "You're stronger than he was. And you wouldn't do that to Claire." A not-so-subtle reminder that he better not think of doing any such thing.

The older man's chin came up, and in his eyes Gage saw a spark of the former SF operator. Strong, determined. "No. Figure I've done enough damage to her already." With that comment he patted Gage's shoulder again and headed for the kitchen.

Gage followed and took the dishtowel from Claire's mother, being as polite as he could under the circumstances, and exchanged a knowing look with Mel, who nodded. He wanted them all out, now, so Claire could decompress without an audience. "I've got this. Y'all go on back to your hotel, try to get some sleep."

She gave him a small smile. "Thanks." Her eyes looked bruised underneath, heavy with the shadows of grief. "Shall we?" she said to her husband. After hugging Claire goodbye, they left. Claire's father followed them a moment later.

Claire hugged Mel, shut the door behind everyone and took a deep breath, her back to him. Gage had already braced himself for her reaction once they were alone and he didn't have to wait long.

Pushing away from the door, she whirled around to nail him with an angry glare. "What the hell was that, ordering everyone out of my house?"

"You were thinking it. I just put it into action."

Shaking her head, she stormed past him to snatch the last few plates and cutlery from the coffee table in the living room then stomped into the kitchen to set them on the counter with a thud. "It was rude."

He followed, careful not to crowd her. "No, *they* were for not noticing they'd overstayed their welcome."

Her caramel-colored hair rippled down her back as she shook her head in irritation. "My house, Gage, my guests. *My* decision."

He walked up behind her to help clear the counter of the dishes Mel had washed and she began wiping a damp cloth over it with sharp, angry movements. Her cheeks were flushed, eyes sparking with temper. He was glad to see the fire in her again, but knew she probably wasn't even aware of what was causing it. His kicking everyone out might have annoyed her, but she was angry about Danny's death and looking to take it out on someone.

He could feel the anger seething inside her, almost feel it pulsing from her in waves as she did her best to repress it. Gage didn't mind taking the brunt of the explosion if it gave her the chance to vent some of the confusion and grief.

When he didn't respond to her statement she stopped to glare at him over her shoulder. "You gonna answer me?"

"What do you want me to say?" He calmly began loading the dishwasher.

Claire stared at him, her mouth falling open. "How about you're sorry, for starters."

"Nope. Cuz I'm not."

That seemed to stun her into silence for a moment. She recovered fast, throwing the cloth down with a fleshy plop to fold her arms across her chest, over her rapidly rising and falling breasts. Her breathing was erratic, her eyes spitting sparks. "Well you should be, because you're acting like an asshole! You come in here and just take over everything without even asking me what I want."

"Okay, what do you want?"

Her chin came up, eyes flashing with a tumult of emotions he couldn't even begin to decipher but was pretty sure he could guess at. "I want you to leave."

"No you don't."

The flicker of anger in her gaze burst into a full on blaze as she rounded on him, pointing an accusatory finger at his chest. "Yes I do! And don't tell me what I do and don't want. Don't. You. Dare." Her voice cracked and she blinked fast, a sure sign she was about to lose it.

Rather than back down, Gage shut the dishwasher door and closed the distance between them, advancing on her until he called her bluff and she took a hasty step back. Her spine hit the edge of the counter and still he kept coming, until he was toe to toe with her and she was forced to tilt her head back to meet his eyes. She swallowed, the sound overly loud in the tense silence. This close he could see the fine tremors in her muscles, hear the uneven catch in her breath.

"Back off before I do something we'll both regret," she warned in a low voice.

"No."

"I mean it, back *off*." She punched the heels of her hands into his chest with surprising force. He didn't budge because he knew she needed this. She was spoiling for a fight and he was more than willing to give her that release.

He leaned even closer, placed his hands on the counter on either side of her to cage her in, all the while holding her gaze. "No," he said again, softer this time.

A spurt of panic flickered in her eyes. She tried to duck out from under his arm but he blocked her easily, pinning her hips with his own. Her head snapped up, those wide gray eyes filled with shock as she felt his erection pressing into her belly. She jerked her eyes away, swallowed again. "Let me go. Right now, Gage, I mean it."

She was strung so tight she was on the verge of shattering. A volcano about to erupt. And God, he'd love nothing more than to incinerate in the ensuing explosion with her. He wasn't worried about her hurting him. Whatever she could dish out, he could take it and more. "No."

His calm tone acted like a trigger. With an inarticulate sound of rage, she twisted and shoved at his shoulders. Gage caught her wrists and quickly shifted her away from the counter, backed her up against the kitchen wall and pinned her there with his weight. He had only a moment for his brain to register the feel of her soft curves molded to him before she began struggling, trying to shove him away. Not happening.

He held her there, refusing to back down. Her teeth were bared, eyes narrowed, breath coming in short gasps. Low, animal sounds came from her throat as she fought and got nowhere. He could tell it infuriated her more that he'd subdued her so easily, overpowered her with his greater strength. Recognizing she couldn't win, after a minute or two she stilled, quivering with fury, every line of her luscious body rigid with anger and outrage. With him so close she was forced to tilt her head back to look into his face. The warm puffs of her uneven breaths bathed his skin.

"Fuck you, let me go," she snapped, her voice ragged, tight with emotion.

Hands holding her wrists on either side of her head, he waited for her to calm down and meet his gaze. At last she did and he could see the turmoil written there. All the anger and pain, the physical need she was trying to hide from him. Her sweet citrus scent, intensified by her increased body heat, swirled around him. He could get drunk on her so easily. Just lean down and put his mouth to the rapidly thrumming pulse in her neck, taste that soft, fragrant skin.

Holding her gaze, he let one heartbeat of charged silence spread between them. Another. Letting her know without words that he was fully capable of keeping her like this for as long as he wanted. His body was primed, begging him to grab her, tear that tight black skirt and top off her and force her to vent everything that was eating at her from the inside, replace it with white-hot sexual release.

The throb between his legs bordered on painful. He shifted his hips against her and bit back a moan at the feel of her against his erection, noting the way her pupils expanded and her nostrils flared. The evidence of her arousal kicked his lust into high gear. Gage forced himself to take a single, calming breath, waited until the roar in his ears subsided. If this was the last time he got to have her, he was going to make it one hell of a goodbye.

Staring straight into her eyes, he released her wrists and murmured, "Turn it loose."

CHAPTER EIGHT

Claire was so lost in the dizzying fog of rage engulfing her that it took a moment to realize he'd let her wrists go and for those soft words to penetrate. When they did and his meaning hit home, the breath halted in her throat. Fight him? As in, *really* fight him? It was ridiculous. He outweighed her by at least seventy pounds of solid muscle and had trained most of his life in hand to hand combat. She didn't want to fight him, she just wanted… God, she didn't know what she wanted. She couldn't fucking *think* with him this close.

His eyes were so blue, so intense. "Do it," he taunted, more forcefully this time. She could practically feel the leashed energy humming in his big frame, every muscle coiled and ready, making her body respond in turn.

Her compressed lungs expanded in a sudden gasp and she drew in a painful breath of air. The pain came rushing back. It hurt. All of it. The funeral, the fallout with what was left of her family, the Taliban cell's threat hanging over her head and being constantly reminded that she'd thrown Gage out of her life. She shook her head tightly, growing frantic, afraid of what she might do if he kept pushing her. Because part of her *wanted* to fight. Something he'd obviously recognized long before she had.

Her heart pounded a hard, frantic rhythm against her breastbone. Her mouth was dry. He was blocking her in, preventing her from escaping and venting her pain in private. She was on the verge of losing control, teetering on the brink and she didn't know how to pull back. Gage was like warm steel against her, the hard length of his erection pressed tight to her belly. She could feel him waiting for her decision, poised and ready for her first move. And she knew he wouldn't back down until she gave it.

Staring up at him through narrowed eyes, her breathing quickened once more. His arms and body caged her so tight there was no escape except to fight. Anger rose, swift and hot. The toxic cloud of emotions closed in, suffocating her in a layer so thick it was all she could do to breathe. A funny sound came out of her throat, a mix of rage and grief that knotted her up inside. Still he refused to ease up. Instinct kicked in. She felt the moment the last of her control snapped, a wire pulled too tight. She attacked.

She twisted to lash out with her fists and knees, screaming her fury. Gage merely grabbed her around the waist and leaned in closer to take away her leverage. Absorbing her blows rather than stopping them. She was too enraged to care if she was hurting him. She kept fighting, desperate to get away from him and lock herself behind a door until she could calm down and vent the ugliness inside her. He wouldn't allow it.

Pushed beyond all restraint, she reared back to take a swing at his jaw. He caught her fist in one hand and pivoted, swinging her around in front of him as he swept her feet out from under her with a well placed shot from his foot. She threw a hand out to break her fall but Gage caught her easily and flipped her so that he took the brunt of the impact, rolling to his side and winding up on the rug in the dim hallway.

Shaken, she scrambled to her hands and knees. He followed instantly, covering her with his weight before she could gain her balance. Trapping her beneath two hundred ten pounds of muscle. There was nowhere to go. Her mind rebelled, but her body was done. She sagged, sucked in air through her nose as her body quivered, then stilled.

Gage was poised behind her, his strong thighs bracketing hers, thick arms braced on either side of her head. Heat radiated from his torso, pressed tight to her back, the thickness of his erection rigid against her buttocks. He was barely breathing hard, completely unfazed by her attempts to get free as he bent his head until his warm breath brushed over the side of her face.

"Better?" he murmured against her ear.

Goose bumps immediately erupted across her skin, a torrent of sexual desire ripping through her, replacing the anger. Her nipples beaded against the cups of her bra, suddenly hyper sensitive to the barest whisper of fabric against them with every breath she took. A hot pulse ignited between her legs.

Oh, Jesus. The position, the feel of him snug against her, so hot and ready, had her about to incinerate. A puff of warm air gusted over her temple as he nuzzled her there with his nose, lips so close to her skin. If she turned her head just a fraction, they'd be kissing. She closed her eyes and focused on breathing, let her muscles relax. It didn't help. A voracious hunger clawed at her, twisted her insides with a pounding ache so intense she shuddered.

Helpless to stop herself, she arched her back and ground her ass against his hips. The resulting jolt of pleasure between her thighs made her suck in her breath. *"Gage."* It came out a raw, hoarse plea.

He went still and cursed under his breath. One strong hand moved to her hip, gripped it tight as he circled his erection against her. So close, only a few layers of clothing separating her from what she needed. She whimpered at the sensual torture. He froze at the sound, bent until she felt the gentle brush of his lips against her bare nape. "Okay, baby. Hold still."

Yes, please, do it. Claire let herself go lax, dropped her head to lay her cheek against the thick pile of the rug. She needed him so badly, didn't care that it was going to be here in the hallway. All she cared about was having him inside her to ease this terrible ache, have him fill her until the emptiness went away, even for only a little while.

Gage shifted behind her slightly and set his palm flat on the rug next to her face. She reached out blindly and grabbed his thick wrist, hanging on tight. Another kiss against her nape, this one harder, the tender stroke of his tongue sending flames licking across her skin. His other hand caressed the curve of her rear, cruising over the tight fabric of her skirt in seductive circles. She pushed back against it, impatient, dying to feel him slide inside her.

A whisper of air brushed her inner thighs as he eased the hem of the skirt up her legs, higher, until the curve of her ass was exposed along with the lacy black strip of her thong nestled between her cheeks. He growled softly, stroked his palm over her bare skin.

"You wet for me?" he murmured against the top of her spine.

She nodded and licked her lips, the hand around his wrist tightening, the fingers of her other hand digging deep into the rug. *Hurry, hurry,* she urged him, her body pulsing with need.

She gasped when his mouth fastened over the sensitive spot on the side of her neck. His tongue licked her in lazy circles as he reached around her hips to cup the dampened lace between her thighs. The heat of his hand, the subtle pressure of it, dragged a soft cry from her. He circled his palm slowly, spreading the moisture beneath the lace with a satisfied growl, and scraped his teeth against her neck. His breathing was erratic and she could feel his heart pounding against her back. She wriggled her hips to get more friction where she needed it but he pulled his hand away to slide over her hip and ease his fingers beneath the band of lace nestled in the valley between her cheeks.

"Are you still on the pill?" he demanded, easing the scrap of lace aside in a slippery caress across her clit that made her shudder and strain back for more.

She shook her head, unable to answer. They both knew there was a tiny risk that his vasectomy might not be a hundred percent effective, but at the moment she didn't care. The need was clawing at her, making her frantic.

Another low curse, then finally, finally she felt the pressure of his fingers against her opening. He slid them up and down her folds, spreading her wetness as he twisted his wrist from her grip and reared up on his knees. She heard the sound of a zipper lowering and almost wept in relief. A second later he planted his hand back beside her head and eased two fingers into her body.

She bowed up at the feel of it, moaned when he rubbed over that hidden ache inside her and withdrew to circle her swollen clit. "There," she breathed, the plea evident in her voice.

"Yeah, I know you like that." He pulled his hand from between her legs and positioned the blunt head of his cock against her. Blood pounding in her ears, Claire held her breath and waited, every muscle in her body quivering in anticipation.

With a firm grip on her hip Gage surged forward, burying himself deep. He felt huge inside her. The sudden fullness, the friction against her inner walls was incredible. Claire bucked in his hold, a wild cry tearing from her lips.

He held firm, stayed locked inside her so that she could feel every pulse of her muscles around him. "Easy, baby, I got you."

That Southern drawl slid over her like warm honey. She made an unintelligible sound.

His teeth nipped the side of her neck. "You're gonna come for me." The words were low, commanding.

She nodded, mindless with sensation, desperate for the release he could give her. Gage didn't make her wait. He groaned and plunged in and out of her, fucking her hard, that hand on her hip holding her in place. Claire widened her thighs and arched her hips as much as she could, seeking just the right angle.

In a smooth motion he eased up into a kneeling position and pulled his wrist free of her grip to slide his hand between her thighs. His fingers slid beneath the front of the thong to find the tight bundle of nerves there and started stroking in time with his thrusts. Her whole body tightened at the brutal lash of pleasure. She gritted her teeth and reared back against his thrusts, riding him as hard as he was her, rubbing her clit against his slick fingers, demanding the release he was pushing her toward.

"Give it to me," he growled.

The impassioned demand launched her. Pleasure rocketed through her, winding tight until it snapped free in a glorious burst of heat and sensation. The orgasm rushed through her in wracking spasms and she was barely aware of her shattered cries echoing off the walls around them.

When it was over she went limp beneath him, her thighs trembling from the effort of keeping her weight balanced on her knees. Eventually she became aware that she was crying softly, one side of her wet face still pressed against the rug. Gage was completely still, locked deep inside her, huge and hot, his breathing labored. She pressed back toward him in a plea for him to finish, but he gripped both her hips and slowly withdrew with a pained hiss erupting from between his teeth.

Fighting to open her teary eyes, Claire risked a look at him over her shoulder. The light spilling through the kitchen doorway bathed the right side of him in a warm glow. He still wore his dress shirt and had his jeans shoved halfway down his thighs, exposing the gleaming length of his cock standing straight out from his body. His face was rigid, nostrils and mouth pinched like he was in agony. She started to reach out a hand to touch him, wanting to give him the same pleasure he'd given her, but he blocked it and wrapped his fist around himself instead. She watched, spellbound as he started pumping, his hips moving in counterpoint to the rhythm of his hand.

He stared directly into her eyes as he stroked himself, letting her see what she did to him, totally unembarrassed by his arousal and need. The muscles low in her abdomen fluttered. Understanding what he wanted, Claire stretched out flat on her belly and pillowed her cheek on her hands to watch the show.

Claire lay flat on the rug with her face turned toward him, watching him silently with glistening eyes. At her wordless acquiescence and approval Gage groaned low in his throat and sped up his strokes, his hand working his aroused flesh.

Fucking hell she was sexy like that, lying there all soft and satisfied from the orgasm he'd given her.

Even wet from tears and with mascara smudged beneath them, those big gray eyes seemed to glow at him in the dim lighting, like banked coals waiting for a breath of oxygen that would make them burst back into flame. She'd been so wet, so tight around him. The way she'd been writhing against him with those sexy little cries spilling from her lips, he'd almost come with her. It had taken an act of will to pull out of her warmth, but having her watch him so hungrily now while he stroked himself was even hotter.

Her gaze swept over his body to where he was fisting himself so tightly. She licked her lips in reflex and he felt his balls tighten. God, it was so erotic to have her watching so intently, like she wanted to eat him up. A few more pumps and he gasped, threw his head back and let go, coming across her bare ass in hard spurts. Claire gasped. He watched his come hit her creamy skin, a fierce possessiveness twining with the pleasure at the evidence that he'd marked her, claimed her. *His.*

In the aftermath he slumped forward to rest his weight on one hand, bent his head so that he could nuzzle the side of her mouth as he caught his breath. God, he was destroyed. His muscles trembled so much he could hardly support his weight on his arm. The moment his mouth brushed hers Claire turned her head and kissed him, parting her lips in a silent plea for deeper contact.

He gave it, sliding his tongue into her mouth to play with hers. Soft and slow now that the insane heat had been quenched. For the moment, at least. With her it always flared fast and hot again in a matter of minutes. Didn't matter how many times he had her, he'd never get enough. Their chemistry was unlike anything he'd ever experienced.

With a soft mewling sound Claire reached one hand up to slide it around his nape. Gage rested more of his weight on his left arm and deepened the kiss, absorbing her sigh of contentment while his heart rate stabilized. After a minute he turned his face to layer kisses over her damp cheek, over her closed eyelid. She rested her head on the back of her right hand and let out a shuddering sigh.

Easing his weight back on his haunches, he stroked the hair away from her temple and expelled a deep breath. Jesus, he was soaked with sweat. His shirt stuck to his back and chest as he tucked himself back into his underwear and did up his jeans.

Claire started to push up but he stilled her with a gentle hand between her shoulder blades. She was all wet and sticky with his come. "Lie still. I'll be right back." He went to the bathroom and dampened a facecloth with warm water, then came back to her and wiped her skin clean.

After easing her skirt back down into place he went to one knee and rolled her onto her side. She reached up for him immediately and he gathered her into his arms, lifted her and strode upstairs to her room. Once there he helped her strip her clothes off and dumped them into the laundry hamper for her. When he came out of the small walk-in closet she was already beneath the quilt, head on the pillow as she watched him.

He stood there, unsure what he should do next, but then she pulled back the covers on the empty side of the bed in invitation. Wanting the comfort of holding her, he slid in beside her, fully dressed, and drew her close. She snuggled into his chest with a weary sigh and he kissed the top of her head, savoring the warmth of her silky soft skin beneath his hands.

"Sleep, baby," he whispered against her hair. Running a soothing hand over her delicate spine, he listened to her breathing deepen and even out. Within minutes, she was fast asleep. Gage closed his eyes and cuddled her close, wishing he could hold her like this forever but knowing it was impossible. After they talked in the morning, he'd probably never get the chance again, so he was going to savor every last moment while he could.

CHAPTER NINE

Claire woke slowly from a deep and dreamless sleep. Her body was sluggish and heavy, the covers warm around her. She became aware of pressure against her spine and hips then a large male hand stroking down her side. Sighing, she snuggled back into Gage with a tiny smile on her lips. Even half asleep, just like always his touch set her nerve endings humming. Her breasts tightened and a heavy throb started between her legs.

The caress of his fingertips stayed slow and easy, spreading tingles in their wake, keeping her drifting in that lovely place between sleep and wakefulness. Enjoying it too much to wake up just yet, she kept her eyes closed and let herself slide into the sensation.

Gentle brushes against the curve of her breast dragged a sigh from her. She shifted and arched her back to give him better access. A moment later a puff of cool air washed over her as he pulled the quilt back. The touch of his lips against her breast sent a wave of heated anticipation through her.

She rolled to her back and slid her fingers through his short hair, urging him on. He obliged, opening his mouth over one beaded nipple and sucked. Her breath hissed through her teeth as pleasure zinged from her sensitive nipple to the

123

growing ache between her legs. Gage cupped her breasts in both hands and took his time pleasuring both tight peaks. When she was squirming and writhing beneath him he shifted lower, trailing a line of kisses across her ribcage to her belly, pausing to dip his tongue into her navel.

Forcing her eyes open, she blinked in the semi-darkness and watched Gage's shadowy face disappear between her legs. The warmth of his breath washed across her wetness and she curled her fingers into his scalp. When they'd first gotten together she'd been shy about him going down on her but he'd quickly destroyed all her inhibitions about her body. He'd made it clear how much he loved pleasuring her this way and she wasn't about to stop him. Her spine arched at that first slow, soft kiss against her heated flesh and a moan slipped out of her.

His hands slid beneath her hips and his shoulders wedged between her legs, forcing them wider apart until she was completely exposed to him. There was no embarrassment for her now, only a liquid heat stealing through her body. He pressed his mouth between her thighs with a low sound of enjoyment and then she felt the first wicked stroke of his talented tongue.

Fire streaked through her. Her head rolled back on the pillow, eyes falling closed as she lost herself to ecstasy. Gage knew exactly how to push her to the peak, exactly what pressure and rhythm she needed, what drove her mindless, and he used it all to his advantage now.

She was panting, gripping his head and rolling her hips against his mouth when he at last worked two fingers into her and searched for the hidden spot that would intensify everything and send her flying. His other hand trailed up to one of her breasts to play with her nipple.

She tightened around his fingers and gently rocked her hips in time to his rhythm, allowing him to set the pace as the tension within her built to the point where she became desperate. His fingers found just the right spot inside her at the same time his tongue softened on her clit and his lips surrounded the swollen bud in a tender, sucking kiss. Her helpless cry of release filled the room, the pleasure cresting and breaking in slow, endless waves. By the time it faded she was limp against her pillow, a soft moan of fulfillment spilling from her lips.

She opened her eyes to look down at him as he raised his head from between her legs. In the gray light seeping around the edges of the blinds she could see how shiny his mouth was, and the heated gleam in his eyes. She reached for him automatically but he sat up and she realized he was still fully dressed. Before she could close her fingers on the buttons of his shirt he leaned away and started undoing them with slow precision, watching her reaction the entire time.

Her lower belly fluttered at the sight of this magnificent man baring himself to her in an erotic striptease. The shirt parted gradually, revealing a few inches of his muscular chest at a time. Claire licked her lips and propped herself up on her elbows for a better view. When all the buttons were undone he shrugged the garment off with a muscular ripple that made her inner walls clench.

He was beautiful, all sleek, delineated muscle with a dusting of red-gold hair across his chest that narrowed to a thin line down the center of his belly and disappeared into the waistband of his jeans. There was just enough light for her to make out the intricate designs of his tattoos that began on his shoulders and ran to each wrist. She clearly made out the Green Beret insignia on his right shoulder, the arrowhead with an upright dagger in its center, overlaid by three diagonal lightning bolts.

Beneath that on the inside of his bicep in a twining script was their motto, *De Oppressor Liber*. To Liberate the Oppressed.

She trailed her fingers over the words, something shifting inside her. She'd come to resent both the symbol and the words in her life but now she couldn't deny it was part of why she'd fallen in love with Gage in the first place. To her his ink was beautiful, a testament to the challenges he'd faced and survived, persevering in the face of adversity. Names of his fallen soldiers, his daughter's on the inside of his right forearm.

He shifted and the light angled across his naked torso. Her eyes snagged on a new tattoo over the left side of his chest. She peered closer, stunned when she recognized her name inked there in a beautiful flowing script, placed right over his heart. She jerked her gaze to his and stared up at him, a knot of emotion forming in her throat. God, that tat undid her completely. He'd permanently inked her name onto his chest even though she'd sent him away and hurt him so badly.

She opened her mouth to speak but Gage captured her hand instead and brought it to his mouth. He placed a warm, lingering kiss in the center of her palm, then settled it over the flowing script and pressed her hand into his skin. *Yours*, the gesture said.

She felt the muscle twitch beneath her palm, the goose bumps that roughened his skin. The need to feel him up against her was so strong she thought her heart would burst if she didn't get to hold him this instant. But when she reached up to wrap her arms around him he shook his head and removed her hand from his chest, placing it back on the sheet beside her.

Before she could protest, his hands went to the fly on his jeans. He released the button and zipper and slowly pushed the layers of denim and cotton away from his lower body. Claire groaned at the sight he revealed. She was still wet from her earlier release, her body once again alive at the thought of feeling him sliding deep inside her. From the amount of heat in his eyes she expected him to grab her legs, hook them over his wide shoulders and plunge into her as deep as he could.

He didn't. His thick erection bobbed under her gaze as he straddled her torso with a knee on either side of her ribs and she felt an answering melting sensation between her thighs as she understood what he wanted.

Hungry for the taste of him on her tongue and the chance to give him the same pleasure he'd so unselfishly lavished on her, Claire licked her lips and closed her hands on his strong hips, waiting. She didn't dare speak for fear of shattering the spell he'd woven.

Holding himself in one hand, Gage eased forward to rub the smooth tip against her mouth. She opened immediately, watching his eyes as he slowly fed the head between her lips. At the first touch of her tongue he groaned deep in his chest, those eyes like blue flame on hers. Again she let him set the slow, torturous pace as he withdrew and pushed back inside, relishing the salty tang of him on her tongue, the way his muscles twitched and quivered each time she sucked or twirled her tongue around the head of his cock.

Gripping his hips tight, she hollowed her cheeks and raised her head to take him deeper still. Gage's thighs and belly tensed, all those hard muscles standing out in sharp relief. His free hand reached out to fist in her hair, applying firm pressure to hold her where he wanted her, remind her that he was the one in control. She made a quiet sound of agreement and relaxed her jaw as he began to thrust slowly in and out of her mouth. Her fingers dug into his ass, holding him close. As the seconds passed she watched his expression turn harsh as the need to come coiled inside him.

His chest rose and fell in a rapid rhythm, the sound of his ragged breathing adding another layer of excitement. She knew he was close when he let his head fall back and closed his eyes, teeth bared against the pleasure she was inflicting. A low, throttled groan rumbled up from his throat. Claire swallowed around him, anticipating the taste of his release on her tongue. His head came up. He met her eyes down the length of his body and the raging desire there sent a shock-wave of pleasure through her.

The hand in her hair relaxed, shifted to her face and cupped the side of her jaw. He started to withdraw but she made a protesting noise and dug her fingers deeper into his flanks. The muscles in his jaw flexed and for a moment she was sure he was going to pull out. But then he relaxed his stance and slid his hand into her hair again, holding her still with firm pressure.

"God, that feels so good, Claire," he whispered. He stroked in and out of her mouth a few more times then went rigid. A light sheen of sweat gleamed on his chest.

Claire sucked him harder and let her tongue play.

"Fuck." Gage's hand contracted in her hair and he stared down into her eyes as he came with a long, drawn-out moan.

She swallowed each pulse until he stilled and relaxed above her. With a gentle caress of his fingertips across her cheek, he withdrew slowly from her mouth and eased to his side next to her. Her lips felt swollen and she loved it. Curling up against him, she kissed the delicate lines of ink that made up her name and rested her cheek there. His arms came around her, holding her tight, his lips brushing her temple.

More content than she'd been in months, she closed her eyes and let herself slide back into sleep.

Gage's heart tripped then went into double time when he heard Claire's footsteps coming downstairs. It'd been almost three hours since she'd destroyed him with her sexy as hell mouth and fallen right back to sleep on him. He'd been careful not to wake her when he'd dragged himself from her warmth for a shower and spent the rest of the time alone rehearsing what he wanted to say, because he knew he'd only get one shot at it.

He was more in love with her than ever, and if she still didn't feel the same way he needed to know. His guts were in knots about what her reaction would be.

She appeared in the kitchen doorway with a tender smile for him and the sight of it took his breath away. Even without make up and wearing plain old jeans and a T-shirt she was so unbelievably sexy he wanted to peel her clothes off and bend her over the kitchen island. But there was more to a relationship than sex, even if it was the best he'd ever had, and the explosive attraction between them had never been the problem anyway.

"Hey," she said, crossing to the counter to help herself to a mug of coffee from the pot he'd made. "I thought you'd still be sleeping. If I didn't wear you out like I thought I did, I must be losing my touch."

"If your touch was any better, you'd have killed me," he said wryly, joining her at the island and sinking onto a barstool there. That tight feeling in his chest wouldn't let up and he recognized the bubble of fear beneath it. If she turned him away this time, what the hell was he going to do?

She sipped her coffee and made a low sound of pleasure, watching him over the rim of her mug with those gorgeous gray eyes. When he didn't say anything, just stared back wondering how the hell to start things, she frowned a little. "You all right?"

No, he was going fucking crazy dancing around this. "Yeah, I'm great." He finally broke eye contact and wrapped his hands around his mug for a second while he gathered his resolve. He'd been both dreading and anticipating this conversation for months. It was now or never. "So…we need to talk."

Her eyebrows went up at that and she set her mug down with a little smile. "That's usually the woman's line, but you're right, we do."

She hadn't closed up on him or gotten all defensive. Yet. Was that a good sign? He cleared his throat, drew in a breath. "What are we doing? I mean, this." He gestured back and forth between them. "Because I'll be honest, I don't have a fucking clue."

Claire blinked at him. "About what?"

Shit, she was going to make him drag this all out of her? "About *this*. Am I just here for you to lean on until you don't need the support anymore? Are we just fucking while we're at it?"

Her eyes flashed with anger. "Gage."

"Well, Jesus, help me out." He needed to know where he stood before he lost his fucking mind.

"All right." She got up and dragged a hand through her caramel hair, the ends curling lovingly over her breasts in a completely distracting way. He forced his gaze back to her face as she paced back and forth across the kitchen and cut him a glance. "You know why I broke up with you."

"Yeah, and as far as I can tell, none of those reasons have changed."

At that she stopped, seemed to wrestle with herself a moment before she met his eyes. "That's true."

His stomach plummeted. His fingers tightened around the mug, suddenly so numb he couldn't feel the heat radiating through the ceramic. For a second he was sure his heart seized. In that moment he couldn't think of a single thing to say.

"It wasn't an easy decision for me, you know."

He stared. Was she joking? She wanted his sympathy or something, for making the choice to leave him? He might have laughed if the whole thing wasn't so damned gut-wrenching. "You ripped my fucking *heart* out, Claire." His whole world had imploded when she'd gone.

She visibly flinched and seemed to curl into herself more, as though the words hurt her. And damned if he'd feel sorry about that. "I know. I know it did and I hated myself for it." She took a step toward him, then stopped. "I'm sorry. You have no idea how sorry I am for that."

He clenched his jaw and forced himself to breathe past the burning in his lungs. There was no doubt her apology was sincere, but he wanted way more than that. Except it looked like he wasn't going to get it. His heart was still beating, had to be since he was still alive and breathing, but he couldn't feel it. It was iced up in the center of his chest, constricted in terror about facing the rest of his life without her.

Clearly distressed, she took another step toward him, might have come around the island to him if he hadn't instinctively leaned back in a gesture of self protection. She paused, looking uncertain, and blinked as though fighting back tears. "You haven't changed," she finally continued in a rough voice, "but I have."

He couldn't speak, just stared at her feeling utterly help-less. He'd given her his heart on a fucking platter the first time and he'd been ready to do it again. What the hell was wrong with him?

She sighed, still visibly distressed by his reaction. "Look, walking away from you was the hardest thing I'd ever done, but at the time I knew I had to do it. I know exactly what sort of man you are, Gage, and so I knew how important your job is, how much your men mean to you."

She shook her head as she continued. "I lived my whole life coming in last with the men in my life, at the end of the line behind God, country and unit. I've lived every day worrying about my father and brother, either when they were training or deployed and it didn't stop when they came back. You know what I've been through with them both at home, especially Danny. I swore I'd never do that to myself again. Swore I'd never get involved with a military guy period, let alone take a back seat to everything else for any man I was in a relationship with, no matter what. I didn't want to settle for that kind of life anymore…" She trailed off, leaving him hanging on the edge of a hellish cliff.

She was afraid, he realized. Afraid that he'd wind up a drunk like her father or killing himself one day like Danny just had. He shook his head slowly. "I'm not them," he said simply, his voice rough. "And you know it."

Something ignited in her eyes. Anger, yes, but also convic-tion. "You're *exactly* like them. You're trained to think and react the same way they were. I've lived my whole life around SF soldiers, so don't tell me I don't know what I'm talking about. You've dealt with everything you've been through unbelievably well so far, but I know how you guys think. And I know you wouldn't hesitate to give up your life for one of your teammates during an operation, just like I know you wouldn't hesitate to take a dangerous job if Tom or one of the other guys asked you to. It's part of who you are and nothing can change that." She stopped and took a breath, folded her arms across her breasts.

"But?" he heard himself croak. There had to be a *but* in there somewhere. It was there in her face. At least, he prayed that's what he was seeing, and not just reading more into her hesitation than he should.

She spread her hands in a helpless gesture, and he caught the sheen of tears in her eyes. "But despite all that it turns out I was wrong," she answered softly. "Leaving you was the biggest mistake I've ever made in my life, and I'm so sorry. Can you forgive me for hurting you that much?"

What? He sucked in a painful breath, afraid his heart was about to explode. "Claire."

She held out a hand to silence him. "No, let me finish. I'm not saying I'm okay with dealing with all that shit again, especially after what Danny just did, but when he died I realized something important."

A long pause followed while she gathered her thoughts and he knew better than to risk saying anything. His heart was pounding, the hope swelling hard and tight beneath his ribs.

Finally Claire swallowed, nodded as if she'd come to an important decision. Her eyes pleaded with him for under-standing, for forgiveness. "At the end of the day, life is too short to spend it being miserable. I knew that intellectually, but now I know it here." She pressed a hand to her chest and he could see she was suffering just as much as he was. More, because this was all compounded by her brother's death. "I was worse than miserable without you. I sent you away because I was afraid of getting hurt and that was stupid because it didn't save me from the pain after all. I don't know how I'll handle everything down the road with you doing dangerous things in your job and all the other issues we haven't resolved, but I do know that living without you hurts way more than any of that."

He was too surprised by that to answer, afraid to move or speak lest it stopped her from talking and ruined everything.

She drew an unsteady breath, tilted her head a little. "So I'm saying that...even though I'm scared and I know it'll be hard and I'll come in last a lot of the time, you're worth it. I love you and maybe I don't deserve it, but I want another chance. If you're willing," she finished in a rush, looking so vulnerable and uncertain it made his chest ache.

Gage could hardly take it all in. *Jesus Christ.* He shook his head, flooded by a relief so staggering he blinked against the sudden sting of tears. If he was willing? Did she have no clue what she meant to him? She was the beating heart in his chest.

He stood up so fast the stool shot back two feet behind him, then he was moving toward her without even realizing it. Two steps across the tile floor, Claire flew straight into his arms. Gage caught her to him and hugged her fiercely, squeezing his eyes shut against the painful swelling in his heart as she returned the tight embrace. Of all the things he'd expected her to say, none of this had even been a possibility. He was humbled by the way she'd laid herself bare to him with her honesty.

"I love you too. Never stopped," he managed roughly, part of him wondering if he was imagining all this. She'd been absolutely unyielding in her decision when she'd cut him out of her life all those months ago. Nothing he'd said or done had made a damned bit of difference, but the tragedy of Danny's death had made her willing to fight for them. This was his dream come true, a thousand times better than anything he'd ever imagined.

His face was buried in her hair. He breathed in the tangy, crisp scent of her and held her in a bruising grip, half afraid she'd vanish if he let her go. What she'd said was stuck in his mind. He rocked her ever so slightly, trying to convey his depth of feeling for her with his desperate hold. "I understand why you're afraid, I do, but you don't come last with me, I—"

His phone rang in his hip pocket. He silently cursed it and thought about ignoring it but his gut warned him it might have something to do with what Zahra had uncovered the other day. The development he hadn't told Claire about yet that the rest of the team had been briefed about in a discreet meeting in the funeral home parking lot after Danny's service yesterday. He'd wanted to shield her from it as long as possible but he couldn't hide it any longer.

"Fuck. I don't wanna answer that, but I have to," he said against the top of her head, her hair silky smooth against his face.

"It's okay. Go ahead," she murmured, stepping back to wipe at her eyes.

No, it wasn't okay. And the instant he found out what whoever was on the other end wanted, they were finishing this conversation. Reluctantly, he eased his grip and let his arms slide from around her, immediately missing the feel of her against his body.

Pulling the phone out, he saw Hunt's number on display and answered. "Hey."

"Hey. How you guys holding up today?"

"We're great." A thousand times better than what he'd imagined them being five minutes ago, considering everything she'd been through over the past few days. "What's up?"

"We got word on the suspect in Baltimore. We know who he is, and half the law enforcement agencies in the region are out looking for him right now. The latest transmission from his contact in Tajikistan said there's a Tuesday night deadline for him to kill the target."

Gage cursed under his breath, his eyes snapping over to Claire. She was back at the island, watching him. She was completely still as she stared at him, her mug poised halfway to her mouth, the alarm in her eyes telling him she knew it was bad news.

"Bring her here until we know more about the situation," Hunt continued. "The more eyes we have on her until this is cleared up, the better."

Fuck yeah, after seeing what the TTP had pulled off in their attempts to get Khalia, Gage wasn't taking any chances with Claire's safety. "Roger that. See you in a little while." He slipped the phone back into his pocket and faced Claire, frustrated that they'd been interrupted in the middle of patching things back together, but hating the reason behind it more. The thought of Claire being in imminent danger made him crazy with the need to protect her.

Her face was pale. "What?" she asked, clearly alarmed.

"I need you to pack a bag with enough stuff to last you a week," he said calmly. There was no way for him to soften the news, not without lying to her. Running a hand over his skull trim, he decided it was kindest to say it straight out. "Looks like the TTP's hired assassin's deadline just got moved up, so for the time being I'm moving you in with the rest of the team for added protection."

CHAPTER TEN

Four hours later Claire pushed her laptop away from her on the kitchen table in the safe house where the Titanium team was staying and leaned back into her chair to rub at her eyes. After such a great start and a promising breakthrough with Gage, the day had suddenly turned to shit and wasn't nearly over yet.

Not only had the threat level gone up substantially in the past few hours, she and Gage had been too busy working with the rest of the team to even begin an attempt at ironing out the remaining issues that had split them in the first place. Her parents both wanted her to meet them at Danny's place to go through his things before her mother left town but with this new threat Claire couldn't come and go as she pleased. And she didn't dare tell her parents what was going on.

Her father knew something was up though, she could tell from the things he'd asked her over the phone. But as long as she was with Gage and the others, she felt safe.

Unable to fight it, she let loose with a jaw-cracking yawn.

Beside her, Zahra cracked a grin. "Wow. Did Gage keep you awake all night *again*?" she teased, gaze fixed on her own screen.

"I'll never tell," Claire answered, though she knew her own smile was answer enough. She stretched her arms over her head and sagged back in her chair with an exhausted sigh. The finality of Danny's death had begun to sink in, making it hard to concentrate. Grabbing some sleep was an impossible dream at this point, though she doubted anyone would mind if she crashed in one of the upstairs bedrooms for a while.

It was only the two of them in here and no one else was within earshot because the guys were out in the living room gathered around the coffee table to talk logistics. When she'd arrived here with Gage, Hunter had surprised her with the news that he'd hired a cleanup crew to go over to Danny's place and take care of everything so her parents wouldn't have to deal with any of that while they went through Danny's things. She was so appreciative of his thoughtfulness. The entire team's, actually.

Everyone had been kind to her, especially Zahra, who'd been trying to keep things light with her considering the intel they'd just unearthed. People thought the linguist was aloof and cold, but Claire knew better. It was all a front, designed to keep everyone at a safe distance. If you earned your way into her trust, you saw a completely different side of her.

"Wish Alex would call and give us something else to do," Claire muttered. She and Zahra had spent the past few hours sifting through more intel while they all waited for word from Alex after he finished an important meeting with several other directors, members of the FBI, CIA and Homeland Security. Alex wanted their team ready to move and staying in the safe house afforded them the best position for now.

"I hear you," Zahra answered, typing away on her keyboard.

Everyone in the intelligence community wanted to find this Mostaffa guy and bring him in before he could strike.

Officials already had a team of FBI agents hunting for him here in Baltimore but his neighbors said he hadn't been home in a few days and nobody knew where he'd gone. Apparently he was the freaking superintendant of his building, and everyone was shocked that he'd done anything bad that would involve him in an investigation. Claire wrapped her arms around herself, still shaken at the thought of being evacuated from her home because she was on a terrorist's hit list.

Driven by morbid curiosity, she clicked on the file on her desktop to bring up his picture, though his face was already permanently etched into her memory. A Caucasian man in his mid twenties, clean shaven with dark brown hair and greenish eyes. Mostaffa was good looking, which for some reason was even more disturbing to her.

According to the background info on him, his parents had emigrated from Tajikistan before he'd been born. His father had worked as a plumber and the mother had stayed at home to raise Mostaffa. A few police reports over the years hinted at domestic disputes that had gotten out of hand, but that had stopped once the father died almost a decade ago. Mostaffa— Mo, as his friends called him—had gone to trade school and worked various jobs in construction, plumbing, gas fitting, and most worrisome, as a technician for ADT Security Systems.

Claire stared at the image on screen, trying to make sense of it all. Though born and raised in the States, somewhere along the way Mostaffa had become radicalized. He had no criminal history or anything else that might point to why he'd joined the Taliban cause. He wasn't even on any of the government watch lists. Likely why the TTP had chosen him.

"Hey, why don't you shut that down and we'll take a break for a while," Zahra said, shutting down her own laptop.

"I can't stand looking at that guy anymore and you need some down time."

"Yeah, good call." She powered down the laptop. The scariest thing about this guy was that he looked so ordinary. Nothing about him stood out and he'd left no suspicious trail online that they could find, no doubt why he'd gone completely unnoticed in the counterterrorism world until the past few days. Made her wonder just how many others there were like him out there, sleepers waiting to be activated by cells both here and abroad. Knowing they existed was one thing; dealing with them firsthand—being named their possible *target* was quite another.

"You hungry?" Claire asked her, needing a distraction from her thoughts.

"I could eat." Zahra eyed the fridge dubiously. "Think they've got anything decent here?"

"Don't get your hopes up." Claire got up to rummage through it. At first all she saw was beer, and plenty of it. She shook her head. As far as she knew the only guy in the house who could cook was Gage, and he was busy in the front room with Hunter, Ellis and Dunphy.

Considering the details of the recent threat, they were all way too paranoid to order something for delivery. That left either cooking or someone making a run to a takeout place, and Claire didn't mind fixing something for everyone if she could find some actual food to work with. It would give her something else to think about besides Danny and the TTP for a little while.

After pulling some chicken and veggies out of the bottom drawer in the fridge, she got busy chopping while Zahra hunted for something to flavor it with.

"All we've got is ketchup and vinegar," Zahra said sadly, placing the bottles on the counter next to the stove.

"They're such guys," Claire muttered. "Just find me some salt and pepper and we'll make do with that." She did a quick stir fry and tossed in some cooked pasta to fill everyone up. Zahra helped her plate everything and they took it to the guys. The men looked up at them as they entered. Gage's intense blue gaze raked over her in a lazy, appreciative sweep, a warm smile lighting his eyes. Her skin tingled in reaction as though he'd physically touched her.

"It's not fancy, but it's better than nothing," she told them, placing plates in front of him and Hunter.

Dunphy—Sean—half turned in his seat to smile at Zahra as she approached. "Hey, thanks."

Zahra plunked his plate down with an irritated frown and didn't look at him. "Whatever, I didn't make it, Claire did. And don't get used to this. Just because I'm a brown girl doesn't mean I like running around serving you guys food."

"Okay, I take back my thanks. How about a plain old fuck you instead?" He picked up his fork and scooped a bite into his mouth, smiling at her as he chewed.

Surprisingly, Zahra laughed. "Just so we're clear," she added, smirking.

"We're clear. I promise to never expect any more hand delivered meals from you."

"Good." Aiming a grin at Claire, she tossed her long dark hair over her shoulder and sauntered back into the kitchen.

"Well, on that pleasant note," Claire said dryly, "I'm gonna go eat with her since she seems to prefer my company to yours."

"Thanks," Gage and Hunter said in unison, already shoveling food into their mouths.

"You're welcome." She smiled at Gage and fought back a pang of longing, wondering when they'd get the chance to continue their discussion. Maybe later tonight after everyone turned in for the night. Once she and Gage were lying in a sweaty, tangled mess in their bed. The man was addictive and sexual chemistry aside, she appreciated having him with her through all of this.

Seating herself at the kitchen table, she raised an eyebrow at Zahra, who studiously ignored her as she forked up a bite of her lunch and shoved it in her mouth. Claire cleared her throat for emphasis.

Zahra's eyes darted up to hers, expression all innocent. "What?" she demanded around a mouthful of noodles.

"Exactly," Claire countered. "You got something going on with Dunphy that I don't know about?"

She snorted and forked up some veggies. "He wishes."

Okay then. Claire hid a smile, enjoying the opportunity to rib Zahra and glad to be talking about something so normal for once. "Just checking, because I seem to recall you saying something about swearing off men for cats for the next six months. Of course this just means I like you even more."

Zahra paused and gave her that cool look Claire had no trouble seeing through now. "What are you talking about?"

Claire knew her co-worker wasn't used to dealing with military types, except for Alex. "I love a woman with a backbone, and trust me, you'll need it to deal with these Titanium guys. That type of alpha male, they have a way of wearing you down after a while. You gotta stay strong." She said it tongue-in-cheek, having just seen the spark between Zahra and Dunphy for herself.

"Oh, don't worry, my spine has no problem telling them where to go and what they can do with themselves once they get there."

Grinning, Claire stabbed a piece of red pepper with her fork. "Glad to hear that." Sounded like she was going to keep

Dunphy on his toes while they worked together, that was for sure.

They were rinsing off their plates in the sink when the man in question strolled into the kitchen carrying a stack of his own. "See, I brought the dishes in here myself, rather than expecting you to come back and get them," he said to Zahra, black eyes dancing with mischief. "Check me out, all domesticated twenty-first century guy and shit."

"Great, you can do ours as well then," she replied sweetly, stepping aside. She passed Claire on the way back to the table, a smug grin on her face. With a grudging chuckle, Dunphy got busy rinsing the plates then loaded them into the dishwasher while Claire watched in approval.

"I really like her style," she said to him, trying not to laugh.

"Yeah, she's got a certain something, doesn't she?" he murmured, watching Zahra start her laptop back up as he closed the dishwasher door. He opened his mouth to say something else, no doubt another smart ass remark, when someone's cell phone started ringing in the front room. Dunphy's was next. Then another. As he pulled his phone out of his pocket, Zahra's went off too.

"Is he calling us in?" Claire asked, assuming it must be Alex. Her own phone was in her purse, over by the front door. Nestled beside the Beretta from her nightstand that Gage had insisted she carry with her from now on. She might not have any law enforcement training or field experience, but a woman wouldn't grow up in a house with two commandos and not know how to fire a weapon properly. Though it'd been a while since she'd gone to the range, she was pretty sure she could still hit whatever she aimed at.

"Looks like," Dunphy answered, reading whatever text message had come through.

Footsteps sounded on the tile floor, then Gage stepped into the kitchen. Though someone else might not have noticed the subtle tension in him, with one look at his face Claire knew something was wrong.

"Alex just called us all in for a meeting. Wants us in the boardroom ASAP," he said.

Her heart thudded at the grim set to his eyes and mouth. "What's going on?"

"We'll see when we get there."

Bullshit. He knew something. He and Hunter both. Did it have to do with her? Had they just found out something about the attack? Zahra was already gathering up her stuff. "Gage, tell me what—"

"Let's go, Claire. Grab your stuff and get in the truck." He turned and walked out without another word. Swearing to herself, she snagged her laptop, hurried to the front door to get her purse, and pulled out her cell phone. She found nothing but the text from Alex, telling them to come in. But she was sure she hadn't misread that look on Gage's face. Had he received a different message than the rest of them? Otherwise Hunter must have said something to him.

Stewing in silence, her trepidation growing by the second, she walked out the front door behind Zahra and climbed into the back of the idling SUV Gage was driving. Whatever was going on, she'd find out soon enough.

Just his luck that the clouds decided to open up as he drove back to the house in the new vehicle he'd borrowed, a silver minivan as inconspicuous as any he could find for this neighborhood. He almost couldn't believe it when he saw the empty driveway, and his heart rate quickened. Parking at the curb out front, he took a look around to make sure no one was watching him. He grabbed his backpack full of tools from the passenger seat, tugged on his thin leather gloves and walked up the driveway.

The house was dark except for the light on in the foyer that he could see shining through the side panel windows on either side of the front door. Once he was sure he wasn't walking into a trap, the first thing he had to do was pick the lock and disable the alarm system. Until he got inside he couldn't tell for sure what he was up against, and there was always a chance someone was still at home but his time was running out and that called for taking drastic risks. At his back, the muzzle of the weapon there dug into his skin, ready if he needed it.

Stealing one last glance around to ensure he hadn't attracted any unwanted attention outside, he tried to look as innocuous as possible as he took out his tools and picked the deadbolt. The lock slid free. Considering his target, he was shocked and a little disappointed by that. This was the point of no return. Mo took a deep, calming breath and cracked the door open. A high-pitched beeping filled the air. No going back now. He shut the door and popped the keypad off the wall, well aware that he had under a minute to disable the system. Sweat broke out on his upper lip as he took out his special pliers and clamped the wires. Another piece of electronic equipment he'd used during his tenure with ADT and a few adjustments later, the beeping stopped. Mo stood absolutely still, hardly daring to breathe as he waited. Was there a backup system he'd missed? Ten seconds passed. Twenty. When the full minute came and went without any sirens going off, he let out a sigh of relief.

Leaving everything in place, he picked up his backpack and checked the lower floor for the utility room. He found a door that opened to a small space with the hot water heater and built-in vacuum system. A flick of a switch and his flashlight illuminated the darkness beyond the vacuum where a kind of trap door was cut into the floor.

Bingo.

Placing the flashlight between his teeth, he slung his pack onto his back and lifted the trap door, exposing the short wooden ladder that extended into the crawlspace. He climbed down it.

The low ceiling was covered in cobwebs, and from their undisturbed state it looked as though no one had been down here in a while. Following the humming sound, he squeezed his way through some of the wooden support struts stabilizing the first floor and found the furnace. A fairly new model, and he knew exactly what to do with it thanks to his former occupation as a gas fitter.

A rush of excitement filled his veins as he took the pack off and emptied out the tools he needed. He made short work of the required tasks and double checked everything before climbing back out of the crawlspace and shutting the trap door behind him. Pausing inside the utility room door, he listened for any hint of sound or movement. Blessed silence greeted him. Without wasting another second he crossed to the front door. He carefully put the keypad back in place, reset the system and closed the front door behind him. He used his tool to lock it again and walked back to the minivan, relief and anticipation flooding him.

Keys in hand, he tucked a small remote into his jeans pocket and hit the unlock button on the keyfob. When he was halfway to the van a vehicle pulled into the driveway next door. Mo recognized the nosy neighbor from the other day and mentally cursed. She was watching him, put on a polite smile when she caught him looking at her.

Returning it, he smoothly walked to the end of the driveway and collected the bags of grass clippings someone had left there, and loaded them into the back of the van. It took care of the nosy neighbor, but he was worried his target might notice the missing bags and be suspicious when they got home. For this to work, he needed them to be completely unaware that anything had been tampered with. Thankfully the neighbor paid him no more attention whatsoever and he slipped behind the wheel with a grateful sigh.

Mo steered away from the curb and circled the block once to ensure no one was following him, then stopped a few hundred yards south of the house and shut off the engine. From here he could still see the house and know the moment his target arrived home, but he was far enough away to afford him the seconds he'd need to escape unnoticed after he made the hit.

Hunkering down in his seat with his ball cap pulled low over his forehead, he settled in to wait for the target to return so he could finish this.

CHAPTER ELEVEN

They all made it through the meeting without falling asleep, though Claire looked ready to pitch face first onto the boardroom table at any moment. Gage shifted and leaned back farther into his seat, trying to mask his annoyance for her sake.

The meeting he'd thought would be so pivotal to this entire investigation had unfortunately turned out to be a total fucking waste of everyone's time. Acting on an anonymous tip that had precipitated Alex's previous meeting with all the agency higher-ups in the first place, the FBI team on scene had reported that the man they'd found was not Mostaffa.

After two hours of useless effort, no one was any closer to knowing the bastard's whereabouts or plans, nor could they find any further trace of him via cell phone towers or credit card info. So far he'd been smart enough to use cash and stay below the radar. For now the investigation was at a standstill and both Alex and Hunter were just as frustrated about that as Gage was.

Alex finally dismissed them all with a brusque command to be back at oh-six-hundred the next morning to get a jumpstart on things. Everyone got up and filed out of the room. In the hallway, Gage waited for Claire and set an arm around her shoulders when she came out. She leaned into him for a second then turned and wrapped her arms around his neck, resting her forehead against his chest with a weary sigh.

He gathered her close and rubbed her back gently, needing to comfort her. "You hanging in there, darlin'?"

"Trying to. Feel like I could sleep for a week though."

"You can crash as soon as we get you back to the house," he promised. Though part of him wanted to grab a hotel room where they could have the privacy they needed to hash out their remaining differences and seal their new bond without anyone overhearing her breathless cries. Arousal swirled at the thought of what he wanted to do to her. The next time he had her naked and willing beneath him, he'd made it very clear exactly what she meant to him, in a way she'd never be able to forget. But that would have to wait. For now, she was safest under the same roof as the rest of the team.

As though she sensed the turn his thoughts had taken, she tipped her head back to meet his eyes. The skin beneath hers was so dark it looked bruised. "I'd rather stay up and talk with you."

He shook his head. "I'm not going anywhere, sweetness. We'll have plenty of time for that talk after you've had a decent night's sleep."

"I'd sleep better with you beside me."

He'd known she trusted him, but hearing those words from her after all their time apart filled him with a gratitude he couldn't express. He lowered his head until his mouth was right against her ear. "I wasn't planning on sleeping anywhere else," he murmured, pausing to kiss the sensitive skin beneath her earlobe and flick his tongue over it. Her breath caught and her fingers sank into his shoulders.

"Hey, get a room, you two," Dunphy remarked on his way past to the elevator down the hall.

"Yeah, let's," Claire whispered to him as she drew back, her eyes flaring with unmistakable heat.

Gage chuckled and bent to kiss her mouth once, not letting her sway him. "You need sleep."

"So take me to bed and make me come first, then I'll sleep like a baby all night."

Her seductive words made his jeans turn uncomfortably tight all of a sudden. "If you're a good girl and do what I say, I might." Her eyes smoldered up at him and he couldn't hold back a grin at her reaction to his intimate tone. She might be headstrong and independent but she loved it when he took charge in the bedroom, adored the rough edge he showed her there. Gage swallowed a groan at the thought of everything he wanted to do to her. "Come on, let's get outta here and find something to eat on the way back." He turned her around and gave her a little push toward the elevator. She shot him a naughty look over her shoulder then caught up with Ellis.

Hunter came out of the boardroom and fell in step with him in the hallway. "Well, that sucked."

"Yeah."

"Let's get outta here and regroup." They rode down the elevator together. Hunter called out to the others as they reached the edge of the parking lot. "Ellis, you go with Gage. Claire, you're with me."

Neither of them gave any indication that the order surprised them, and Gage didn't argue with him. Three minutes later he was in the passenger seat with Ellis behind the wheel of one vehicle, trailing Claire and Hunter's SUV. Though he'd rather be the one with Claire, he trusted Hunter's skill and judgement and felt comfortable that she was in good hands.

"So, what's the plan?" Ellis asked him in his calm, straight forward way. That easy going but alert demeanor was one of the things Gage liked best about the sniper.

"We'll head back to the safe house. Zahra and Dunphy are staying behind to work on some more chatter from recent phone transmissions and the TTP's favorite online forum."

Ellis glanced over at him, speculation in his hazel eyes—more gold than green. "What's your gut say about the shortened timeline?"

"That somebody's in a hurry all of a sudden." And he didn't like it. A desperate attacker was bound to be even more unpredictable, which made them harder to catch and increased the likelihood of collateral damage. When they found this asshole and took him down, Gage wanted that damage kept to a minimum.

The more he thought about it, the higher his level of unease became. This whole situation didn't feel right, although he couldn't pinpoint what exactly was bothering him so much. The looming deadline, the missing link about who was feeding the TTP inside info, their team currently split up with Dunphy back at NSA headquarters.

When they finally arrived at the outlying suburban neighborhood and turned onto the safe house's street he noticed the empty driveway right away. The yard waste bags were missing, and as far as he could tell no one else's had been picked up on the entire street.

The warning bells in his head were now jangling like a fire alarm. Last time they'd been this loud he'd been with a patrol entering a mountain village high up in the Hindu Kush Mountains. Listening to his gut and pulling back to wait for aerial recon had saved his life and the lives of his soldiers that day.

"Hold up," he said to Ellis. The former sniper cast him a sideways glance at the urgency in his tone but didn't say anything as he pulled over to the curb and kept the engine idling. Gage contacted Hunter via the radio. "Something's off. Hang back for a bit. Ellis and I'll check it out."

"What's up?"

"Someone's been here since we left. Not sure if it means anything yet, but I'll let you know. Stand by."

"Roger that."

At his hand signal Ellis steered into the driveway, parked, and they both climbed out. The family in the house beside them were just exiting their garage, the parents each carrying a young child to the waiting car in their driveway. Gage nodded at them and the woman smiled back.

"Your yard looks good," she called out. "That landscaper did a great job."

Gage stilled. "What landscaper?" Ellis remained silent next to him, his attention focused on the neighbor.

The woman blinked at him, shifted her baby on her hip. "The man who cleaned up the yard. He came by a couple days ago when the landlord called him in for a quote."

Tom hadn't said anything about it, and he would've mentioned it to Hunter at least so they wouldn't have accidentally taken down some poor unsuspecting bastard looking around the yard. "You saw him?"

At the sharp edge in his tone she frowned, her eyes growing worried. "Yes, and he was just here a couple hours ago to take away the bags. Is there a problem?" She glanced up at her husband in confusion. "I thought…"

Ignoring whatever she said to her husband, Gage contacted Hunter over the radio. He could just barely see the second SUV parked at the far end of the street. "Did you hire a landscaper?"

"Negative," Hunter replied in a hard, suspicious tone.

Shit, that's what he'd thought, and it meant their cover and location had been burned. "Copy. Stand by." Ellis was on alert beside him, already scanning the safe house for anything unusual. "What was he driving?" Gage asked the woman.

"Um, a silver minivan. I can't remember what kind. He loaded the bags into the back before he left."

"What did he look like?"

"White. Mid twenties maybe? Not as tall as you. Slender. Dark hair." She chewed her bottom lip, her eyes bouncing between Gage and her husband, who was listening closely.

"Any facial hair?"

"No and he was wearing a ball cap. The team with the capital n and y on it. Yankees?" She glanced up at the husband for verification.

Sounded a lot like this mysterious Mostaffa they were try-ing to nail, and Gage's insides tightened. He wished he had a picture of the bastard on his phone to show the woman. Part of him wanted Hunter to get Claire the hell away from here but the other part suspected the slippery asshole was long gone by now. "How long was he here, do you know?"

"I'm not sure. Not long though, maybe fifteen minutes or so because I noticed the minivan parked at the curb on my way upstairs to the laundry room and he was just leaving as I came out to take Eric to swimming lessons." She nodded toward the toddler in the father's arms.

Gage relayed the info to Hunter and asked, "You going to check it out with Tom?"

"Damn straight, but I can tell you right now he didn't call anyone in."

"Yeah, got it." They had to get the team's equipment and sanitize the location, then relocate to a new and undisclosed safe house. "What do you want me to do?" Though he was pretty sure what Hunter was going to say.

"Check it out, find out if the house is still secure."

"We're gonna have to go dark after this," Gage said, knowing they'd have to move even if nothing inside the house had been tampered with. Staying put was too much of a risk now, for Claire, for the team, and the entire taskforce.

"That's affirm. I'll talk to Tom and let you know."

"Roger. I'm out." Gage focused back on the couple who were looking at him with identical expressions of alarm. His pulse slowed as it always did when he was in combat mode, every sense on full alert. "Look, I need you to go back into the house and stay there until I give you the all clear," he told them.

They both froze, staring at him with wide eyes. "Why, what the hell's going on?" the father demanded, putting a protective hand against the back of his son's head and pulling him in close. He backed up a step as if he was thinking about bolting for the car and peeling away. Which, in Gage's opinion, wasn't a bad idea at all. "Should I call the cops?"

He was eyeing Gage's tats now, looking nervous and probably thinking he and Ellis were drug dealers or gang members. "Not yet. It's probably nothing, but I'm going to err on the side of caution. We're with a private security firm working for the government," he explained, gesturing to Ellis. It wasn't much, but he had to say something to reassure these people they weren't thugs about to start a war in this quiet neighborhood. "Go on inside now, and I'll let you know when it's safe to come out."

The couple hurried back into the house and closed the garage door. The moment it shut Gage withdrew his weapon and started up the safe house's driveway, on high alert. "Take the other side and meet me around back," he told Ellis and they split up.

Together they swept the backyard, visually checking the windows and doors. There were no footprints in the wet grass, no damage to anything that he could see, and no evidence that anyone had tried to climb through a window or gain access to the roof. Ellis confirmed the same.

"Stay here and cover the back," Gage told him. "I'll check out the front door." If someone had been skulking around the place for fifteen minutes unobserved, there was no telling what—if any—surprises he'd left behind. Before they went in, Gage had to make sure nothing had been tampered with. If anyone was hiding in there he didn't want them bolting past him or Ellis and escape, and he didn't want to ask Hunter to come back him up because it would leave Claire undefended if anything went down.

With Ellis holding position in the backyard Gage made his way around the right side of the house, hugging the wall, weapon at the ready. On the front step, he saw the faint outline of a damp footprint on the painted wood surface. His gaze darted up to the door, looking for other signs of a break in or maybe a tripwire. He found nothing, and through the side panel window next to the door he saw that the green light on the alarm keypad was still on but Gage wasn't taking any chances.

"I don't see anything, but I don't like the feel of this so I'm not gonna breach yet," he said to Ellis via the earpiece. "Gonna take a closer look. Stand by." Only when he'd determined whether the place was booby trapped would he make the decision about whether to call in backup before they swept the house.

"Copy that. No movement back here."

Maintaining his vigilance, Gage set a hand against the wall and leaned in toward the side panel window to get a better look inside.

Something was up and it was making her damned nervous. They should've all been inside by now, relaxing. Instead Hunter had her well back from the safe house and Gage and Ellis hadn't given the all clear yet. And despite his calm exterior, Claire knew Hunter was on full alert. His posture was tense, his eyes watchful. Her nape tingled in warning.

"What's going on?" she demanded, half turned in her seat so she could see the safe house behind them a block and a half down the street. The neighbors had been talking to Gage and Ellis a minute ago, then they'd bolted back into their garage and closed the door like a rabid animal was chasing them. Gage and Ellis had disappeared into the backyard. Now Gage had come back around the front of the house, only this time she could tell from the position of his arms that he was holding a pistol in his hands.

What the hell? "Did they find something?" Her heart rate accelerated. If Gage was in any danger, she wanted backup for him at least.

"We're not sure yet. Apparently there was somebody there earlier posing as a landscaper." He gave her the description and he didn't have to spell it out for her: they thought it might be Mostaffa. Her skin prickled in alarm.

"Gage is going in to check the place out just to make sure it's secure before we clear out our stuff and find a new location to set up in."

He sounded so calm and it pissed her off. Gage was going in there alone with his freaking *weapon* drawn. Shouldn't Hunter be out there to help? "If you want to go back him up, I'm okay here by myself."

He made a negative sound. "Ellis has his back. They don't need me. We'll just sit tight for the time being."

She hated that he could hear everything the others said via his earpiece while she was left in the dark. Swiveling around to glare at him, she realized he was keeping careful watch on the place via the side and rearview mirrors. Not wanting to disturb his concentration, she forced herself to take a deep breath and sit still. Her gaze strayed from the view in the side mirror out her window to the street and the occasional car that passed by them. None of the drivers remotely resembled Mostaffa and she began to relax slightly.

Then she noticed a silver minivan. Claire focused on it instantly, squinting to make out the driver more clearly as it approached. A man, wearing a ball cap. Hunter's gaze was turned away from it, his attention riveted on what was happening at the house. The van came closer, revealing the driver's face and the Yankees symbol on the front of his hat.

A wave of cold crashed over her, turning her blood to ice. "*Hunter.*"

He snapped his head around, followed her gaze just as the van passed them. "Fuck."

Before she could move, Hunt put the SUV into gear and wheeled it around to follow the van, tires screeching. A block ahead of them, the van slowed.

"Get in the back and stay down," he ordered as he hit the gas and gunned it.

Claire unbuckled her seatbelt and dove into the backseat. Hunter was already on the radio to the others. "Gage, come in—"

He'd barely gotten the words out when an explosive roar split the air.

A scream lodged in Claire's throat at the deafening noise. Hunter hammered the brakes. Claire slid across the slick leather surface to slam into the backrest of the front seat as the concussive force of the blast shook the big vehicle. Cracks appeared in the windows in spider web patterns. Through the blood rushing in her ears, she heard Hunter swear and start rattling off orders to whoever he was talking to. Car alarms were going off everywhere around them, set off by the force of the blast.

Gage! She got to her hands and knees, raised her head and risked a look at the safe house, terrified of what she'd find.

From all the way back here she could see the column of black smoke boiling into the sky from the front of the house. The front door appeared to be lying on the lawn, torn right off its hinges. The windows were blown out and a sheet of flame burned inside the lower floor windows.

"No, oh my God, no," she cried, lunging for the door handle with shaky hands. She yanked on it, discovered it was locked and fumbled with the lock. Through the SUV's fractured windshield she saw the silver minivan was long gone.

Hunter yanked out his earpiece and snatched up the walkie talkie on the console, drawing his weapon with his free hand as he shot out the driver's side door. "Give me status," he barked.

Claire dove into the front seat to grab at her purse on the passenger floorboard. She was frantically digging her pistol out when she clearly heard Ellis's voice respond a moment later, and his response stopped her heart in her chest.

"Gage is down."

CHAPTER TWELVE

Claire shoved the passenger door open so fast she practically face planted onto the asphalt as she fell out of the vehicle. Desperate to get to Gage, she scrambled to her feet and took off running toward the burning safe house, gun in hand. Her heart stuttered when she saw Ellis carrying him across the street over one broad shoulder to set him down on the lawn, but she didn't slow. All she could see was the blood on his face and upper body and it filled her with terror that it was taking so long to get to him.

"Gage," she cried, his name torn from her throat, her legs like rubber as she flew along the sidewalk. People were coming out of their homes to gawk at what was happening, talking on or snapping pictures with their cell phones. Ellis was hunkered next to Gage's supine body with his fingers beneath his chin and Claire realized he was looking for a pulse. A hot rush of tears flooded her eyes and her legs almost gave out. He couldn't be dead. She wouldn't survive that. Didn't want to.

Ahead of her, Hunter charged over and knelt beside them, blocking her view of Gage. Panic flared, hot and sharp. She raced past onlookers and over someone's lawn, heedless of the plants she trampled. Reaching them at last, she dropped her weapon, skidded to her knees beside Gage and scanned his body. The damage she saw sucked the air from her lungs in an anguished cry. Her hand flew to her mouth in horror.

"He's alive," Hunter told her firmly, all his focus on Gage as he and Ellis checked him over.

She blinked the tears away and bit down hard on the inside of her cheek, afraid to touch him or get in their way. Blood trickled out of his nose, mouth and eyes. The left side of his face was reddened, the cheek raw, singed by the heat of the blast. But his chest was still going up and down and that reassured her.

Swallowing her fear, she found her voice. "Gage. Gage, can you hear me?" He seemed barely conscious, his breath coming in broken gasps. His eyes cracked open a bit and she leaned over him, desperate to get him to look at her. She cupped the uninjured side of his face, hoping her touch and voice could anchor and soothe him. "Baby, I'm here, I'm right here. Can you hear me?"

In answer he shifted, tried to move but both Ellis and Hunter restrained him. She could see he was gasping, struggling for air.

"He can't breathe," she cried, but Ellis and Hunter had already seen that and were rolling him to his side into the recovery position. She reached for his shoulders, not knowing how to help him aside from what his teammates were already doing.

Ellis gripped the neckline of the scorched shirt, ripped it down the center and pulled it away, exposing Gage's blood-streaked chest. He swept Gage's mouth with a finger to try and clear his airway, but Gage continued struggling to breathe. He flailed one hand out weakly to push Ellis's fingers away. Claire moved in to cradle his head in her hands, feeling utterly helpless. She dimly heard Hunter talking on the phone in the background, giving medical information to someone and realized he'd called 911. Her eyes tracked each jerky rise and fall of Gage's chest, ready to pounce on him and do compressions if he quit breathing.

"His vitals are good," Ellis said to her as he checked some of the puncture wounds on Gage's skin. They were scattered across his arms and torso, all trickling blood. How far in had they penetrated? Had something hit his lungs? "I know his breathing sounds bad, but his color's okay. He's still getting enough air."

The words took the barest edge off the sharp panic swirling inside her. Her heart pounded sickeningly against her ribs. "What about his head?" Was it cracked? Did he have brain damage?

"He got thrown onto the grass, so he was lucky there." Ellis reached down to pry Gage's eyelids open, one at a time. "Pupils are responding. So far, so good."

It didn't look good from where she was sitting. Aside from that feeble attempt to push Ellis away, Gage was still mostly unresponsive. She had to stay calm. Hunter had called for help and people up and down the street must have too after the blast. It was just that everything was taking too goddamn long.

A black duffel bag dropped to the grass next to her. She blinked up at Hunter. He kneeled and started emptying the medical supplies inside it.

"Hold this," he told her, handing over a thick wad of gauze bandages. Grateful for something to do other than panic, she took it and gingerly dabbed it against the raw spots on Gage's face. His eyelids flickered. He made an unintelligible sound and tried to sit up.

"No, stay still," she said quickly, setting a hand on his shoulder where she was pretty sure it wouldn't hurt him. He didn't listen. Just set a hand on the ground and tried to push up. "Gage, no. You're hurt. Please just stay still." She was terrified his lungs would stop working if he shifted too much. There might be internal damage they couldn't see.

"You're gonna be okay, man, but listen to Claire and lie still," Ellis said and set a hand on Gage's sternum to keep him down. "Paramedics are on the way."

Gage made an irritated growling sound and obstinately pushed up onto his right hip despite all of them telling him not to move.

"Jesus Christ he's a stubborn son of a bitch," Hunter muttered, reaching out to steady Gage, clearly recognizing that he had no intention of lying down. Claire moved in behind him to bolster his upper body but he swatted a hand at Hunter and gave him a menacing scowl.

"Glare all you want, you hard-headed bastard, you just got blown all to hell in that explosion," Hunter fired back.

Gage shook his head as though to clear it and wiped at his eyes, ignoring all of them. "I'm good," he wheezed and at the sound of his voice Claire closed her eyes for a second as relief slammed into her. "I'm good, lemme up."

Hunter and Ellis exchanged an uncertain look and finally eased back a little. Gage propped himself up on one elbow and managed to get to one knee.

"Seriously?" Claire demanded, growing frantic. "You guys are gonna let him get up?"

"He'll either get up or drop trying," Hunter said, his tone filled with a grudging respect that Claire couldn't appreciate at the moment. "Better to get out of his way and see how he does."

This was ridiculous. The man had just been blown up five minutes ago, he couldn't possibly be strong enough to get up.

"Gage, *stop* that." Of course he didn't listen. "What about internal injuries?" she snapped at the other two.

"We'll find out soon enough," Hunter muttered, pushing to his feet. The wail of distant sirens broke the stillness and Claire felt a small measure of relief. Maybe the paramedics could strap him down to a gurney until they were sure he wasn't going to kill himself by moving around like this. Or better yet, tranquilize him so moving wasn't even an option.

Gage was doggedly up on one knee now, still sucking in air. He was bleeding from dozens of little gashes across his chest, probably from flying glass and other debris, and she could already see bruises forming beneath his skin. God, he was a total mess. The burns on his face looked painful and had to hurt like hell. Why wouldn't he just lie down? He managed to get both feet underneath him, though he wobbled a bit. Claire automatically shot out a hand to grab his upper arm and for a moment she was sure he would shake her off like an angry dog but instead he turned his head and looked straight into her eyes.

"I'm all right," he gasped out, loudly, though the effort of speaking clearly cost him. He was pale, way too pale for her liking.

"You're not all right," she snapped, on the verge of tears again. "Your fucking *ears* are bleeding."

He frowned and stared at her mouth and she realized he couldn't understand her because he couldn't *hear* her. The explosion must have blown his eardrums, which would explain the blood coming out of his ears. She shook her head at him sadly, some part of her admiring his toughness despite herself, while the other part wanted to strangle his stupid alpha male ass. "Your ears," she shouted, pointing. "Bleed-ing."

He swiped at his nose and ears, looked away like it was no big deal and did a visual sweep of Ellis. "You okay?" Ever the Team Daddy, always thinking of his guys, even in his current state.

Ellis shook his head in exasperation. "I'm fine, you stubborn prick. Now lay your ass down and let us take care of you."

Gage just shook his head, his bloodstained lips thinned in that unmistakable flat line that meant he'd never give in.

God. Claire stepped around in front of him to get his attention and set her hands on either side of his head, taking in the battered and scalded state of his face. She was so grateful he was alive, but scared out of her mind about how badly he was injured. "We don't know how bad you're banged up inside. *Please* stay still until the paramedics can check you. For me, Gage. Please?"

He reached one hand up to curl around her wrist in a gentle grip she was sure he meant to be reassuring and shook his head. "Eardrums are shot...my chest is tight but I'm...okay otherwise. Promise."

She stared at him, wanting to shake some sense into him. How could he promise something like that? "If you hurt yourself worse because of this, so help me, Gage—" She cut herself off before she could finish that thought and let her hands drop, swallowing the tears in her throat. God, she was shaky as hell, wanted nothing more than to curl around him, protect him and ease the pain he was so intent on hiding. She also knew he'd never let her do it. Not with his guys around and the danger still looming. Mostaffa had taken off in the minivan somewhere but he had to be close by unless he'd ditched it and stolen another vehicle.

Bending to rummage through the medical supplies, she came up with another bandage and started wiping at the blood drying beneath his eyes, nose and mouth. God, it made her feel sick to know he'd almost been killed a few minutes ago. Her hands shook as she did her best to clean him up.

At a gentle touch beneath her chin, she glanced up. Gage was watching her, his blue eyes filled with understanding and tenderness. Yes, tenderness, even though he was the one bleeding all over and in pain he'd never admit to. "It's fine," he said.

She swallowed and looked away from his gaze, struggling to hold it together. More than anything she wanted to hug him, feel his arms around her to reassure her he really was okay, but there was no way to do that without hurting him. "No it's not," she whispered, aware that he couldn't hear her.

Hunter spoke to her. "Emergency crews are almost here. You okay alone with him for a bit? We're gonna go secure the perimeter before the cops get here," he said in a loud enough voice that Gage would hear. "Claire and I saw Mostaffa drive by just before the bomb went off."

"Plate number?" Gage got out, pausing to gasp for a second. Claire wanted to scream at him. He shouldn't be worrying about any of that right now.

"Only a partial," Hunter answered. "He must've remote detonated it when he saw you by the door."

"Fucker," Gage snarled, hands curling into fists. The veins in his neck seemed to be standing out and his color wasn't right, pale from shock and pain and hopefully nothing more serious.

"You guys wait here," Hunter said to Claire, handing Gage the pistol Claire had dumped on the grass before he and Ellis took off across the street. Even in this state she knew Gage would defend her to the last if Mostaffa or anyone else attacked. Sighing, she looked away from him and realized for the first time that a large crowd of onlookers had gathered on the sidewalk in front of them, everyone gawking at the burning house and Gage.

She slipped her hand into his and held on tight and he squeezed back, bending over a little to ease his breathing as he watched Hunter's and Ellis's progress across the street. She could feel the heat of the fire all the way over here and the acrid tang of smoke filled the air. Gage's big body was tense, the shakes already lessening, and for one moment she thought he was determined to go after them. Claire opened her mouth to yell at him, ready to tackle him if he dared try it.

Thankfully he didn't, instead staying beside her with the gun in his hand and it suddenly dawned on her that he wasn't staying put because of his injuries; he was staying put and wouldn't leave her side because as far as he was concerned the threat wasn't over yet. He was on full alert, still guarding her in spite of what had just happened to him. God dammit, he was going to make her cry again. She held his hand and ran her free one up and down his back, wishing there was something she could do to help.

Ellis and Hunter were across the street directing the crowd back from the safe house and doing an initial sweep of the property when the first responders finally arrived. Police cruisers roared up and cops swarmed the area. One officer came over to her and Gage to help and she filled him in on what had happened and explained that they were working for the NSA, while others talked with Hunter and Ellis and worked to get all the bystanders back to a safe distance in case another device went off. Gage's ID was in his wallet but hers was back in her purse, on the floorboard of the SUV she'd been in with Hunter.

When the ambulance arrived Gage was none too pleased about being herded toward it but she and the cop assisting her gave him no choice. He flat out refused to get on a gurney though, and stubbornly sat on the tailgate while the paramedics checked him over. She stood back a ways with the officer and overheard one of the medics say something about a chest tube.

The cop shook his head, eyeing Gage in a kind of awe. "What branch did he serve in?"

Claire expelled a long breath. "Army."

He gave her a cynical look. "No way he's regular Army."

"Nope, no way," she agreed, not caring to elaborate though with his shirt off the cop must have been able to see the SF tattoo on Gage's arm.

"Looks like the door took most of the blast for him. If he hadn't been standing behind it when the bomb went off…" He shook his head. "He's damn lucky to be alive."

"I know." Looking across the street at the ruined door lying on the front lawn, her stomach pitched. "But I still want to shake him until his teeth rattle."

Concealed in the back of the garage in a yard one block over, Mostaffa waited until the third set of sirens arrived before he worked up enough nerve to leave his hiding spot. He pulled his hoodie up over his head to help disguise his appearance. He'd ditched the Yankees hat in the van he'd abandoned four blocks over after he'd triggered the bomb. After darting through a yard down the street from the target house he'd walked to this new location, careful not to draw attention to himself.

The device had gone off exactly as planned, though he didn't know how many of the team members he'd managed to catch in the blast. Now he had to find out and make sure whoever he'd hit was dead, so he could start making plans to take out the others. He had no idea how he was going to do that with the amount of risk he was facing, but he'd rather be taken out cleanly in a fight with the remaining team members than die a slow and hideous death at the hands of the man who'd hired him.

He checked his gun one last time, ensuring he had a round chambered, then ducked out from behind the garage door. His running shoes were silent against the pavement as he turned onto the sidewalk and approached the chaos ahead, falling in with a line of people walking down to see what all the commotion was. All up and down the street, crowds of onlookers stood around on the sidewalks and neighboring lawns. Police were everywhere.

He ducked lower into his hoodie and stuffed his hands into his pockets, ignoring the way his heart was trying to pound its way out of his chest. Fire trucks were already on scene and at least one ambulance. From this distance he couldn't tell if anyone was in the back of it, let alone what state they were in.

He slowed, hanging back a safe distance until he could judge if it was safe to come any closer. The burning safe house stood empty, orange and yellow flames licking at the blown out lower floor windows. A bomb squad vehicle lumbered past him down the road and parked near the main body of the crowd where the police were keeping everyone away from the scene. He watched the black-clad bomb technicians climb out and talk to the other officers already there. No doubt they were here to assess whether it was safe for the firemen to attack the flames.

He noticed a light brown haired woman in a red sweater standing apart from the crowd, near the ambulance. Something about her was familiar. Drawing nearer, he caught a glimpse of her profile and recognized the female who worked for the NSA. Not one of his listed targets, but important nonetheless because of her connections to the rest of the team. The others had to be close by; they would never leave her unprotected.

As though she felt the weight of his gaze, she turned her head and made eye contact with him. Her eyes widened in recognition and his steps faltered. Then her mouth opened and she raised a hand to point at him as she yelled something.

Shit!

Mostaffa started to spin around, ready to bolt. Out of the corner of his eye he caught a glimpse of someone in the back of the ambulance standing up. His gaze locked on Mostaffa like a heat seeking missile and he felt his insides shrivel at the rage and determination in the other man's eyes. Gage Wallace, the Titanium team's second-in-command and one of Mostaffa's highest priority targets, along with Hunter Phillips, the team leader. Wallace had been right by the door when Mostaffa had hit the remote, yet he wasn't dead. Hell, he was still freaking *standing*.

Swearing, Mostaffa took off and veered between two houses. At the end of the first lawn he risked a frantic glance over his shoulder and was stunned to see Wallace coming after him, gun in hand. Two big men and a few cops were right on Wallace's heels. Mostaffa swerved into the nearest yard and ran headlong for the wooden privacy fence at the back. Reaching it, he grabbed the top with both hands and vaulted himself over it, landing with a bone-jarring thud on the damp grass on the other side. Something popped and buckled inside his right knee and he went down.

Stifling a cry of pain, his ribs and shoulder took the brunt of the impact as he hit the ground, costing him precious seconds he didn't have. Terror and adrenaline flooded his system. Fear drove him back onto his feet and forced him onward in a running limp as he crashed through the shrubbery to aim for yet another fence. A dog started barking in the next yard, the high-pitched yapping adding another lash to flay at his frayed nerve endings.

They were coming. He could feel them, gaining on him with every second. Lunging upward, his hands closed over the top of the latticework in the fence. His muscles bunched as he hoisted his body up. He'd just thrown one leg over the top of it when a shout from behind him froze him in place.

"Stop or I'll shoot!"

Unable to help himself, Mostaffa looked back. A big man with dark hair stood where Mostaffa had just fallen at the last fence, a black pistol in his grip, his gaze narrowed on Mostaffa's hands. He knew that face. The team leader, Hunter Phillips. Icy fingers of fear plucked at his spine. The man's posture and expression screamed death. Before Mostaffa could move, another man vaulted over the fence. Light brown skin, deadly demeanor. Blake Ellis, former Marine scout/sniper.

Mostaffa knew he was a dead man.

Fear paralyzed him, sapping the strength from his suddenly unresponsive muscles.

"Get down on the ground and put your hands over your head," Phillips growled, stalking ever closer. Ellis mimicked his movements on the other side, boxing Mostaffa in. He could hear other men coming, shouting in the distance. There was no escape except over this fence, and with his knee already swelling in his jeans he knew he didn't have a prayer of getting away. His hand twitched, ready to go for his weapon tucked into his waistband.

"Hands up," Ellis barked. "Get on the ground, now."

"Hands!" Phillips barked.

They wanted to take him alive, he realized with sudden clarity. But he knew what would happen when they took him into custody. There was no way he was letting that happen.

In that split second decision, he reached back and withdrew his gun. An instant later two bullets hit him in the chest. He didn't even have the breath to scream as he toppled from the fence and slammed into the grass on his back. The pain was so intense it robbed him of breath, an agonizing burn that blotted out light and sound. Somehow he found the will to force his eyes open. The two men were still poised across the yard, watching him with weapons up, ready to fire. He realized dimly that he no longer held his gun. But he did have something else.

Choking on the blood he could feel welling up into his mouth, he forced his hand toward the front pouch pocket of his hoodie.

"Hands where I can see 'em," the commanding voice rang out.

His numb fingers closed around the remote, managed to curl around it. He couldn't see anymore, could only pray this would work. With his remaining strength he urged his shaking arm to pull his hand from his pocket.

"Bomb!"

Before he could draw another breath, more bullets slammed into his chest. He collapsed onto the wet grass, the remote slipping from his numb fingers, then blackness slammed down.

One of the cops smashed a section of the privacy fence in just as the two double taps rang out, four shots in quick succession. The final shot didn't come, telling him someone had held off on the standard head shot.

Gage stumbled forward through the opening in the cedar fence, one arm slung across the shoulders of another cop as the man steadied him. His attempt at running had damn near killed him. He was still shaking, sucking wind and his chest hurt like hell, a damn sight more than the scalded side of his face. Before him in the yard stood Hunter and Ellis, their backs to him, weapons raised. Mostaffa lay flat on his back near the rear privacy fence, bleeding from a grouping of center mass bullet wounds.

Shit. They needed him alive.

"Get a medic," Hunter yelled back at them. He approached Mostaffa with Ellis at his back, kicked something out of the tango's hand. Gage let go of the cop and hurried forward as fast as he could given his shitty breathing. Hunter whipped his shirt off and stuffed it against the bullet wounds while Ellis checked Mostaffa for a carotid pulse. He looked over at Hunter and shook his head. Hunt swore and started chest compressions through the bloodstained shirt, though there was really no point. Even if a medic had been standing right beside them, there was fuck all he could do without starting a transfusion instantly.

Shifting his gaze away from the downed terrorist, Gage focused on what Hunt had kicked from the guy's hand. Something small and black lay in the grass. Squatting down, he examined the remote, aware that this little piece of plastic and circuits had damn near killed him earlier.

"Shit," Hunter muttered, sweat rolling down his face as he kept up with the compressions. "Where the hell's that medic?"

"Too late, man," Ellis said, easing back onto his haunches. "He's gone."

The cops swarmed the yard. Hunter let out a vicious curse and kept going for another few seconds before Ellis reached out and stopped him. Hunter snarled in disgust and stood up, running a bloody hand through his hair. "Fuck, we needed him for questioning. God *dammit*."

Gage walked over and pointed to the remote. Hunter's gaze shifted up from the device into Gage's face. He shook his head in disbelief. "How the hell'd you get here, anyway?"

"Piggybacked," he gasped out, jerking a thumb over his shoulder at the cop who'd helped him. The rest of them were securing the scene, taking possession of the body and questioning Ellis. Hunter would be next, but at Gage's wisecrack the team leader's harsh features transformed into a broad grin.

"Hardcore, man."

"Yeah." Shit, he barely had the strength to stay upright now. "Give me...a ride back... so I can... see Claire?" He paused to wheeze in another breath, clammy all over and shaky as hell. Chances were good he was worse off than he'd thought. "She's probably...freaking out." She'd been screaming his name as he'd tried to chase after Hunt and Ellis. Hell, she'd no doubt run after him before one of the cops stopped her to keep her back. He wouldn't be surprised to walk out of this yard and find her standing there on the sidewalk, waiting to throttle him in front of everyone.

Hunter shook his head in a kind of fond resignation, clapped a solid hand on Gage's shoulder. "You're not going anywhere except to the hospital in the back of that ambulance. And that's an order, even if I have to sit on your chest to make you stay put."

He grinned, pulled in a pained breath. Already felt like he had an elephant sitting on there, he didn't need Hunt's added weight as well. "Look after...Claire for me."

Hunter smirked and motioned to someone behind Gage. The paramedics. "You should be more worried about what she's gonna do to you when she sees you next. She was pretty upset when you took off after the tango. Last I saw she had two cops holding her down on the ground."

He winced. "Shit." He was so gonna get it.

"Scared of your woman, Gage?"

"She's gotta…temper." And she wasn't afraid to use it, at least with him.

Hunt snickered. "Then you'd best get your ass on that gurney they're bringing before she shows up, huh?"

"Yeah." He allowed them to get him on the stretcher, but only after he climbed onto it under his own power.

CHAPTER THIRTEEN

Zahra sat alone in the conference room at NSA headquarters, working on the last bit of translation Alex had asked her to finish before leaving for the night. Most of the team had left over an hour ago, except Sean and she hadn't seen him since he'd disappeared around the same time with Alex to work on something else. Her stomach rumbled, reminding her that it was dinner time and she hadn't eaten since that stir fry Claire had thrown together back at the safe house.

She finished translating the last of the Pashto and Urdu in front of her, shut down her laptop, and stood to stretch out her lower back and legs. Her right leg was giving her trouble again, the muscles stiff and painful from her being stuck in a seated position for so long. She eased her right outer thigh and hip into a stretch, grimacing at first then sighing in relief as the pain faded. The conference room door swung open, startling her.

Sean strode in holding his cell phone in one bronzed hand. The man was as delicious as ever, just under six feet of dark, muscular sex appeal. But his usual smile of greeting was missing, and the set expression on his face sent a wave of unease through her. She straightened and faced him, hiding a wince as the muscles in her hip continued to protest. "What's wrong?" Though she didn't know him well she could tell something was definitely not right.

The muscles in his lean jaw flexed for a second as he stared at her. He seemed genuinely upset. "Someone blew up the safe house and Gage with it. They're transporting him to the hospital by ambulance right now."

Zahra's eyes widened and her stomach sank. "Oh my god, I'm so sorry." Without thinking she dropped her usual guard, closed the distance between them and slipped her arms around him in a comforting hug. She didn't expect him to return it but he did, spectacularly, squeezing her tight against his hard frame and pressing his cheek against her hair. His unexpected response shocked her into stillness. The warm, woodsy scent of him rose up to tease her, her body flooded with a barrage of endorphins from the feel of him so hard against her. He felt and smelled amazing. Too amazing.

Pulling back, she cleared her throat and searched his eyes. He had gorgeous eyes, so dark they were like espresso, but this close she could see the warm flecks of chocolate in them. "What happened? Is he going to be okay?"

"Mostaffa rigged the furnace into a bomb and waited for the team to go back to the safe house. Hunt and Claire saw him driving by, started to chase after him when he remote detonated it. Hunt and Ellis got him but the cops and FBI aren't gonna get anything out of him because he's dead."

That twisted bastard, she fumed. She wasn't a bit sorry he was dead. In fact, she hoped he'd suffered excruciating agony before he'd died. "What about Gage?"

"Hunt said he was conscious and even tried to run after the guy when Claire spotted him in the crowd, the stubborn dumbass. He's banged up pretty bad and they're pretty sure he has at least one partially collapsed lung."

That sounded serious enough to be scary. "What was he doing trying to chase after him in that condition? Claire must have lost her mind." Zahra shook her head, incredulous.

"She was pretty mad but she went with him in the ambulance. I'm going up to the hospital to meet everyone."

"I'll go with you." Since it belonged to the company she left her laptop and files on the table and grabbed her purse. There was nothing sensitive in the papers and no one would be able to access the information on her laptop without either her or Alex's codes. When she turned back she saw the hint of a smile playing around the edges of Sean's full lips, softening his grim expression.

"What?" she asked, wondering why he was staring at her like that.

"I'm glad you're working with us, that's all. Real glad." His voice held a smoky edge that she found incredibly sexy, her vow to become a reclusive cat lady notwithstanding.

She mentally shook herself. "I'm glad to help. I just wish I'd have found something in time to stop the attack." They'd been so close to cracking the case. God, poor Gage. She couldn't imagine what Claire was feeling right now, but Zahra was going to be there to lend her a friendly shoulder to cry on if she needed one.

Sean shrugged, the leather of his jacket creaking. "You tried your best. We all did. Come on." He nodded toward the door and held it open for her. Stepping past him into the hall with a murmur of thanks, she drew up short when Alex and Evers appeared at the end of the corridor.

"We were just coming to get you," Alex said to her then looked at Sean. "You tell her?"

Sean nodded. "She's coming with me to the hospital." He urged her forward gently with a hand on the small of her back. That simple touch caused a spike of heat to radiate out from his palm into her muscles and across her skin in a series of tingles. It felt so good she didn't pull away.

The earlier stretching had helped somewhat but her hip was still stiff, making her gait more awkward than usual. Though she tried to mask it Sean's gaze swept down the length of her body in quick assessment before coming back to her eyes but he didn't say anything. Come to think of it, none of the team members had asked about her limp and she was glad because she didn't want to talk about it. Alex knew everything, of course, because he was her boss and he'd been very thorough with her background during the interview process. It meant he knew exactly how much she wanted to help rid the world of Islamic extremists and their brainwashed, backward beliefs.

"We'll meet you there," Alex said to Sean as he and Evers fell in step with them and walked toward the elevators. He waved to his assistant, still at her desk. "Go home, Ruth. See you in the morning."

The sixty-something woman waved and answered with a tired smile, looking relieved to be sent home for the night. "Okay. Good night."

Alex punched the call button for the elevator and waited for the car with hands on hips. Sean stood to the side with Zahra, his hand still against her lower back and she liked the feel of it there too much to draw away. After a moment Alex shook his head and looked over at her and Sean. "From this moment forward we're going to have to take increased precautionary measures."

"Such as?" Zahra asked, guessing he meant more than simple security measures and sensing there was more to this than he was letting on.

Those silver eyes hardened like steel. "Besides Evers and the rest of the team, the only other people who knew the safe house's location work for the NSA," he began in an ominous tone, the words sending a shiver of foreboding up her spine. "That means whoever leaked it to Mostaffa's contacts was one of us."

Zahra's gut tightened. She hadn't even thought of that, she'd been too caught up in the news about the bombing and Gage being injured to consider such a thing. The elevator arrived and Alex and Evers stood back as Sean ushered her inside with that guiding hand low on her back. As the doors slid shut, the reality hit home that they had a traitor in their midst.

Maybe even someone in this very building.

It took four excruciating hours before Claire was finally left alone with Gage in his private hospital room. The entire crew had shown up after Gage was admitted, including Tom and Hunter's girlfriend, Khalia, who was now on her way to DC for a convention. Dunphy and Zahra had shown up with Alex and Evers. Zahra had sat with her and Khalia until Mel and Claire's parents had both arrived. They'd all waited with Claire in the waiting room while the doctors had inserted a chest tube into the side of Gage's ribcage to re-inflate his collapsed lung and then performed a battery of tests on him.

The X-rays showed no visible fractures in his ribs or skull, although he wasn't in the clear yet because they were still waiting on the final word about the CT scan on his brain and internal organs. Due to the concussion he'd suffered and the risk of more possible symptoms developing in the next few hours the doctors were keeping him at least overnight. And Gage wasn't happy about it.

He shifted again on the uncomfortable hospital bed and she could tell from the disgruntled look on his face that he was feeling caged and in a lot more pain than he'd told the nursing staff. "Will you please just take some of the pain meds the nurse left you?" she pleaded, loud enough to ensure he heard her.

His gaze shifted to her, full of annoyance, his eyes even bluer with all the dark bruising around them from the concussion. The right side of his face was still raw but they'd put some antiseptic cream on him and dressed the worst of the scorched skin with a bandage. Beneath the pale blue gown he had on, his whole chest was covered in cuts and bruises. At least his breathing was back to normal. "I've been hurt worse than this before," he grumbled. "It's nothing I can't handle and I just want out of this goddamn bed."

He wanted out of the hospital period, but that wasn't happening. Even if she had to tie him to that bed with restraints to keep him there. "The more you bitch and the more trouble you are, the longer they'll keep you," she pointed out, at the end of her tolerance for his male bullshit.

Gage glowered at her, like a kid pouting because he didn't get his way. "This is fucking stupid."

Stupid? Really? Sighing, she stood and walked to the window that overlooked the parking lot to get a grip on her emotions. It was dark out now, a bright half moon hanging in the clear night sky. Everything was so calm out there. Made it twice as surreal considering the hell they'd been through today. She'd come so close to losing him forever. So close. Her throat tightened.

"Claire."

Schooling her features into a calm mask, she turned her head to look at him. "What?"

He reached out a hand, his expression contrite. "Come here." He said it so softly, his deep voice holding that intimate tone she couldn't refuse, let alone ignore.

Crossing to him, she sank down carefully onto the edge of the mattress close to his hip and slid her hand into his. Gage closed his fingers around hers and stroked his thumb over the back of her knuckles in a soothing gesture. "Talk to me."

She looked up into his battered face. "About what?" What did he want her to say? She was barely holding it together as it was.

"I know you're scared. Tell me how to make it better."

She looked away to the window, gave a humorless laugh. "Of course I'm scared. This is everything I was always afraid of with you and it came true right in front of me today. And there was nothing I could do to help you. Not a damn thing," she finished, her voice catching.

His grip tightened on her hand. "Hey, I'm tough, darlin'. I can take a lickin' and keep right on tickin'."

She didn't find his attempt at humor amusing. Not in the slightest. It made her so angry that he wanted to joke about this. Edgy, restless, she pulled her hand free and stood, pacing back to the window.

"Bad joke," he murmured with a sigh. "Just trying to lighten the mood."

Claire shot him a glare over her shoulder. "It's not funny, Gage. We still don't know if there's more damage—"

"There's not. Trust me. Like I said, I've been laid up worse than this. I've busted my eardrums before, broken bones and fucked up both my knees. This is nothing."

Jesus, she didn't even want to think about all that happening to him. She ran a hand through her hair, searching for the right words. "You don't understand." He never really had, and that was the crux of the problem. "You don't know what it was like for me today, to see you that way. God, Gage, when I saw Ellis carrying you across the street I thought you were dead. I can't...I don't know how to handle this on top of everything else."

His frustrated sigh was amplified in the quiet room. "So now you're having second thoughts about us again?"

Looking back at his damaged face, seeing the bruises and bandages in the gap where the hospital gown gaped in the center of his chest, she wanted to cry. It was hell, loving a man like him, just as she'd known it would be. But was she willing to walk away again? "No. I'm just...I'm scared," she admitted.

He exhaled as though in relief and let his head lean back against the pillow, and she realized he'd actually been afraid she'd leave him. That she'd walk out of the hospital and out of his life, for good this time. Her chest ached that he'd thought she might. She'd hurt him so badly before.

He raised a hand again, the one without the IV line plugged into the back of it, and beckoned to her. "I know, and I get it, I do. Come back here and let me help with that."

This time she didn't hesitate. Her love for him was stronger than the fear and always would be. Two steps from the bed, his cell phone buzzed on the rolling table beside him. He glanced over at it distractedly then back at her, still holding out his hand, prepared to ignore it.

"You'd better check that," she said. "Just in case." Might be Hunter or Tom with more news. With Mostaffa dead, they were scrambling to connect the threads and find out who he'd been working for. And with the threat of a mole within the NSA itself, the stakes were high for everyone.

She wrapped her arms around her waist as Gage relented and reached for the phone to check the display. "It's Janelle," he said, and answered. "Hey, baby girl. You'll have to talk real loud because I can't hear too well right now."

Claire stayed where she was while they talked, warmed by the obvious love he held for his daughter. It hadn't been easy for him to repair the damage to their relationship, but he was trying, and he was sincere about the effort. Luckily Janelle sensed that and was willing to reciprocate.

After a short pause in the conversation Gage frowned and fidgeted in the bed. "Aww, come on now, don't cry," he said gruffly, clearly discomfited. Claire could just imagine what Janelle was saying, and she was glad. He was getting a taste of what it felt like to have someone you love be in pain and not be able to do anything about it, let alone fix it. Maybe from his daughter's reaction he would realize just how much they loved and worried about him.

He raised his head from the pillow a long moment later and Claire could see the torment in his eyes. "Yeah, she's right here. What? No, just repeat that last part because I didn't catch it… Okay, hold on." He held out the phone to her. "She wants to talk to you."

Claire took it from him, made sure her voice was calm and steady when she spoke. "Hi, honey."

"*Claire.*" The teenager's voice cracked. "Oh my God, I couldn't believe it when I got your message. Is he really all right? He said he couldn't hear and that he's fine but I know Dad, he could be dying and not admit how bad it is. So you tell me what's really going on because I know you won't lie about it."

She smiled at that. "He's doing a lot better than he should be," she allowed. "His eardrums ruptured but the doctors said they'll heal and he should recover most of his hearing. The rest of him's just really banged up and so they want to keep him at least overnight to make sure nothing else is wrong." It was a miracle he wasn't in critical condition as far as she was concerned. "Unfortunately for all of us, he's being a giant pain in the ass about it."

"I'll bet." Janelle took a deep, shaky breath and let it out again, obviously battling through tears. "I was so scared he was gone."

"I know, me too. But he's still with us."

A sniffle. "I'm just starting to get to know him again. He's really gonna be okay?"

"Yeah, he really is." *This time.* She silenced the vicious little voice in the back of her mind with a mental slap.

"Thank God." Janelle cleared her throat. "So are you guys…are you back together? Or what?"

Claire didn't want to get the girl's hopes up, but she wasn't going to lie, either. "Yeah, we are." And in so many ways that scared the living hell out of her. "Hope that's okay with you."

"Hell yeah, it's okay," Janelle retorted. "God, I prayed every night for weeks that you'd take him back. He was totally miserable without you. Like, for real."

Claire studied Gage as she answered. "He was?"

"Totally," Janelle confirmed. "And I know you really love him, so I'm glad. Dad deserves someone who makes him happy."

Dammit, she was going to cry again. She swallowed before responding. "Thanks, honey. That means a lot to me to hear you say that."

"Welcome. Will he be going home with you once the doctors release him? Because Mom said she'll pay for my flight up there if I can come for a visit. Please? I really want to see him."

"We'd both love to see you too, but I don't really know where we're going after this." She certainly couldn't go back to her place now that the team's safe house had been destroyed. They were all going to have to go off the grid for a while. "Wherever it is, I'll let you know, okay? I have a feeling I'll need the backup. He's not a very good patient."

"I know, he's the worst! Can I talk to him again? I wanna say goodnight."

"Of course you can. See you later, honey."

"Bye, Claire. Thanks for taking care of him for me."

Her heart turned over at the wistful note in Janelle's voice, the little girl longing for her father and wanting to help take care of him. "You don't ever have to thank me for that."

"Well, I still want to. Give him a hug from me."

"Will do. Here he is."

To her surprise Gage's eyes held a sheen of tears as he took the phone back. He blinked fast and his voice was rough as he continued his conversation with his daughter. When he finished and set the phone aside he expelled a long breath and winced, putting a hand to the spot where they'd shoved the catheter between his ribs. "Damn, I hate that she was so upset. Both of you."

Claire eased down beside him again and leaned down to gently wrap her arms around his wide shoulders, resting her head beside his on the pillow. She closed her eyes when he slid his arms around her back to return the embrace. "This is from Janelle," she said softly next to his ear.

He squeezed her in reply, telling her he'd heard her. "What about you? Do I get one from you too?" he murmured against her temple.

Nodding, she slid up higher on the bed until she could lean in and press her face into his neck. Even with the antiseptic scent of the hospital on him, he still smelled like Gage. She thought her heart might burst with gratitude at the feel of him pressed up against her, alive and whole. She savored every point of contact between them, every rise and fall of his chest and beat of his heart.

"Love you," she told him fiercely, her mouth close to his ear. He was worth any fear and pain that came along with him.

"Love you too. C'mere." He tugged her closer, pulling against her resistance until she was stretched out on her side beside him and her head was nestled into the hollow of his shoulder. The hospital gown dipped lower, exposing the top of his chest. In the dim light cast from the streetlights outside, she could just see the top of her name inked into his skin over his left pec. She traced it idly with one finger, careful to stay away from the nicks that covered his skin. The nurses had spent over an hour picking glass out of him and they said there'd probably be more working through his skin in the coming weeks and months.

Gage kissed the top of her head and ran a soothing hand down her back. "You told me you don't want to come last in my life, but you never have." She stayed very sill, listening to each word he said, sensing he'd been thinking about this for a long time. "I love my daughter a thousand times more now because I wasn't the greatest dad while she was growing up and I know I'm lucky that she even wants me in her life now. And yeah, I love my job. But you're just as important to me as they are. More so, in a lot of ways. Hell, Claire, I *need* you. Need you more than I've ever needed anyone. My life was fucking empty without you in it."

Her finger stilled its motion on his chest. It was rare for him to talk about his feelings, let alone with this sort of honesty or raw emotion. Her throat tightened. "I need you too."

His hand pressed harder against her back, as though he needed to feel more of her against his body. "You know I won't be able to do this kind of work for much longer," he said at last.

She finished tracing the L, moved on to the upward arc of the A. "Yes you will." He'd wind up running and maybe owning a company like Titanium one day.

"No, I mean out in the field. I'm almost forty three."

"I know," she said wryly. "That dozen year age gap between us never gets any shorter, old man."

"Eleven and a half years," he corrected, same as he always did.

"Close enough."

His chest rumbled in a muted laugh. "I'm not letting you use that as an excuse to talk yourself out of being with me, by the way."

"Nah, I've decided to let that one go."

"Thank Christ for that. But I meant that my body's taken a lot of punishment over the years. I still want to be out there with the guys placed under me, but I think maybe it's time that I…scaled things back a bit."

Claire lifted her head to stare at him. "Scale it back how?" Her heart beat faster, hope rising swift and painful inside her.

He toyed with a lock of her hair that had fallen over her shoulder. "I mean maybe I can work more behind the scenes unless there's something specific they need me for out in the field. Hunter's part owner of Titanium now and with how many new contracts Tom's taken on, he's hinted that he could use a hand with running the company."

"Are you doing it for me?" She had to ask. As much as she wanted him out of harm's way, he'd resent her later on down the road for pushing him out of action before he was ready.

"Well, partly, but I've been thinking about it for a while now. I wouldn't want to leave the guys completely when they're running ops, because I've spent most of my life doing that kind of work. I'm not ready to give all that up yet. But I am willing to take a step back. It's time."

Claire kissed him. Set her hand against the uninjured side of his face to cradle his cheek in her palm and settled her mouth over his. "I love you," she murmured, "no matter what you do."

Gage made a rough sound and slid his fingers into her hair to cradle the back of her head, deepening the kiss. "You won't run out on me this time?" he muttered against her lips when he pulled back an inch.

"No," she vowed, meaning it and surprised by how good it felt to say aloud.

"Even though I'm way older than you and I have a teen-age daughter and I can't have any more kids and I do dangerous shit for a living?"

At one time she'd convinced herself that Janelle and his vasectomy were yet more reasons why they couldn't be together, but now she realized how stupid she'd been. She wanted Gage more than she wanted anything, even the chance to be a mother. Maybe somewhere down the line they could talk about adoption but if not, it wasn't a deal breaker for her. Being a stepmother to Janelle was a bonus, not a burden, and she hoped they could form a close relationship from now on if the girl was willing. "Nope. No running," she promised, smiling against his lips.

"Good because I wouldn't let you go again anyhow." Gage grinned and tucked her head back down against his shoulder, cuddling her close. "Gonna marry you, you know."

A joyous smile broke over her face, her heart swelling. "Are you?"

"Yeah. You didn't know, but I bought a ring back in March."

He had? Stricken, she sucked in a pained breath and started to lift her head to apologize but he held her fast against his shoulder. Warm lips nuzzled the bridge of her nose. "Gonna go talk to your dad and ask for your hand as soon as I get out of this fucking hospital, then go pick up the ring."

She loved his old fashioned manners. Her father would be deeply touched by that gesture of respect from Gage. Man, would she love to overhear that conversation. "You kept the ring?"

"Yeah. I wasn't ready to give you up completely. Guess some part of me never stopped hoping I'd get another chance to convince you I'm the only man for you."

She closed her eyes and smiled against the hospital gown. "You *are* the only man for me." She couldn't wait to be Gage's wife. "And if you want out of this place sooner rather than later, then I guess you'd better be on your best behavior and do what they tell you, huh? Starting with taking your meds."

"Yeah, you're right." His sigh was full of resignation. Then he squeezed her once and kissed her forehead. "Pass me those pills then, baby, because I want to slide that ring on your finger by tomorrow night."

CHAPTER FOURTEEN

Four days later

The first thing Gage noticed when he woke was that he was alone in his bedroom at the Outer Banks. He was acutely disappointed by that until he smelled the scents of brewing coffee and frying bacon drifting up from downstairs. He sat up and climbed out of bed, feeling much less stiff than he had when he'd left the hospital in Baltimore three days ago. The cuts on his chest were healing and the bruises were turning from purple to yellow, not nearly as sore as they had been. The side of his face was already growing new skin, though he'd probably have a bit of scarring despite all the vitamin E cream Claire insisted on slathering on him every day.

After a hot shower to ease the aches and pains even more, he threw on a T-shirt and a pair of jeans and headed down the narrow staircase to the main floor of the beach cottage. His shoulders almost brushed the walls as he descended but he didn't want to make any major structural changes because his grandfather had built this place with his own hands and Gage wanted to preserve it.

At the bottom of the stairs the tang of salt and thyme wafted in from the open window above the kitchen sink.

Beyond it, the Outer Banks lay bathed in the warm September sunshine. Bright morning sunlight filtered through the French doors he'd installed that summer, opening up the tiny space to a gorgeous view of the rolling waves hitting the beach a few hundred yards away.

If he strained hard enough he could hear the muted roar they made. His ears had healed to the point that his hearing was already improving and that fucking annoying ringing had pretty much stopped.

The sight that greeted him in the galley kitchen made his heart swell.

At the stove stood his two girls, their backs to him, chattering away while they flipped pancakes and added the finished ones to a platter waiting on the counter beside Claire. Her sapphire engagement ring sparkled on her left hand as she grabbed the ladle and poured batter onto the sizzling hot griddle. Janelle had her red-gold hair pulled back into a ponytail and Claire's caramel-brown hair was loose against her shoulders. They stood hip to hip as they cooked and were so into their conversation that neither of them heard him enter the kitchen. They both craned their heads back when he came up behind them and settled his arms around their shoulders.

"Mornin'," he murmured, pressing a kiss to the top of Janelle's head and then bending to cover Claire's lips with his own. She tasted like orange juice, sweet and tangy, and he went back in for another sample.

"Ew, okay, come on," Janelle muttered, wiggling out from under his arm to attend to the cooking pancakes. "Can you guys tone it down in front of me? I'm only here for a couple days, you should be able to manage it no problem."

"This is toned down," Gage told her, smiling as he thought about the last time he'd eaten pancakes with Claire in this very kitchen, months ago when she'd practically attacked him and stripped him naked right in front of the stove.

As though she was remembering it too, Claire turned pink and smacked his arm while Janelle shook her head, but he noticed his daughter was smiling. She'd made it very clear that she approved of the impending marriage and she and Claire had spent hours going through wedding dress magazines over the past two days since she'd joined them. They had another two days with her before Janelle flew home to her mother's, then he had one last day alone with Claire before they were both due back to Baltimore to work with the Titanium team and the rest of the taskforce to find the NSA mole and bring down the fucking cell that had nearly killed him. The team had since learned that the assassin had planned to take out him, Hunt, Ellis and Dunphy. Mostaffa had acted on orders from the contact in Tajikistan, who in turn had acted on orders from the man who appeared to be directing the TTP cell, Malik Hassani, former head of intelligence for the Pakistani ISI.

When he and Claire got back to Baltimore, they had a lot of serious shit to contend with.

Until then he planned to enjoy his time with his girls, because getting away here was good for all three of them. Claire was still grieving for Danny and the change of scenery had been the best thing he could have given her. And when Janelle left, he and Claire would spend their last day enjoying the beach, then he'd rediscover every sensitive spot on her delectable body with his hands and tongue without worrying about anyone overhearing the sensual cries he pulled out of her. Gage loved his daughter, but he couldn't wait to be alone with Claire again.

"You hungry?" Claire asked him.

"I'm always hungry around you."

Janelle made a strangled sound and turned from the stove with a huff. "Seriously? Hello, I'm right here. God, talk about scarring your kid for life." She grabbed a plate and helped herself to bacon and pancakes, poured syrup all over everything and headed for the French doors. "I'm gonna go eat out on the deck so you two lovebirds can have some privacy before I lose my appetite."

The doors shut behind her and Claire shook her head at him in consternation. "You really should watch teasing her like that. I don't want to make her uncomfortable."

"Trust me, she loves how affectionate we are around her. She told me last night during our father-daughter walk on the beach that she's happy about us and excited for the wedding, especially since you asked her to be a bridesmaid."

Her smile lit up her whole face. "She said that?"

"Yes, ma'am." He reached out to run his fingers through her soft hair, loving her all the more for how willing she was to make Janelle a part of her life. Their life. "I know walking into being a stepmother isn't easy, but so far you're handling it like a pro."

"Well." She ducked her head and glanced away, that pleased smile still in place as she ladled more batter onto the hot griddle. "I'm not going to try and force anything, but respect is a two way street. I figure I'll just give her time and let things develop naturally, then hope for the best. It's an adjustment for us all, but I know we can do it. She's a great kid, which helps."

"That's her mother's doing." While he didn't have much good to say about his ex, in the parent department he had to give her an A plus. God knew he hadn't been the best husband while they'd been married.

"Oh, I'm pretty sure it's your doing as well. She worships the ground you walk on, in case you haven't already noticed."

"I made a lot of mistakes with her and her mom, and I'm the first to admit it. But I've learned my lesson and changed a lot so I won't make them again, I promise."

"Better not, otherwise I'll beat your ass," she muttered, but he caught the way her lips quirked as she said it.

Grinning, Gage wrapped his arms around her waist and pulled her back into his body while he looked out the French doors. From his vantage point he could see Janelle's profile, the end of her red-gold ponytail trailing over one shoulder. His daughter was a beauty, and it would only be a matter of time before the boys came sniffing around.

He shook his head. He could hardly believe he was the father of a teenage girl. Now that was some poetic justice, right there. "I'm glad you'll be with me through whatever comes next with her. Because I have a feeling I'd better get busy cleaning all my rifles."

Claire laughed and flipped the pancakes. "Oh, you're gonna be *that* dad, huh?" She chuckled. "I love it. I can see you now, out in a rocker on the front porch with a rifle and some gun oil, polishing up the barrel when her date comes to pick her up."

He could see it too, and the fucking horny little bastards showing up at the door better not even think about setting a finger on his baby girl before she was twenty one. "I know how teenage boys think," he grumbled.

"You mean that they have sex on the brain all the time like men do?"

He grinned and pressed his hips against the lush curve of her ass, already growing hard at the thought of what he'd do to her later on tonight once Janelle was asleep in the guest room. If they could wait that long. "You love that I think about sex all the time."

"Only because you're so good in bed." She eyed him over her shoulder, those sexy gray eyes sweeping over his chest. "And anyway, all that strenuous bedtime exercise sure seems to have helped you heal fast."

"It's all about incentive with me," he murmured, bending to nibble at the side of her neck. He smelled her warm, sweet fragrance, savored the little catch in her breath and the scattering of goose bumps that rose on her skin. If he slid his hand under her shirt, he knew he'd find her nipples hard and pressing against the cups of her bra. He'd never experienced such explosive chemistry with anyone but her and he looked forward to enjoying it as often as possible.

Claire slid the most recently finished pancakes onto the platter, but there were still a few ladles of batter left in the bowl and he didn't think he could wait that long. "How hungry are you right now?" he purred, sliding his hands up to cup her breasts. "Can breakfast wait while you come upstairs with me for a while?"

She tilted her head back and opened her mouth to reply but instead he watched her eyes darken with desire when she saw the hungry look on his face. "We can't. Janelle's going to come back inside any minute and she'll know what we're doing."

Gage glanced outside and smiled. "Nah. She's on her iPhone now. We've got all kinds of time." Enough to pin Claire to the bed and make her beg to come before he finally relented and sent her over the edge. "I mean, if you can keep up with me."

In answer she quickly reached out and turned off the stove. "Race you to your room, old man."

Gage barked out a laugh and released her, then gave her a few seconds' head start before chasing up the stairs after her on silent feet. He couldn't wait to spend the rest of his life with her, but right now he was going to remind her of some of the perks that came with taking an older, more experienced husband.

—The End—

Complete Booklist

Titanium Security Series
(romantic suspense)

Ignited

Singed

Burned (late 2013)

Bagram Special Ops Series
(military romantic suspense)

Deadly Descent

Tactical Strike

Lethal Pursuit (September 2013)

Suspense Series
(romantic suspense)

Out of Her League

Cover of Darkness

No Turning Back

Relentless

Absolution

Empowered Series
(paranormal romance)

Darkest Caress

Historical Romance

The Vacant Chair

Acknowledgements

Another big thank you to my support team, Katie Reus and my hubby Todd. Your constant encouragement means so much to me and I appreciate the gift of you both being in my life! Love you guys.